THE FIRE BUG CONNECTION

Also by Jean Craighead George

Animals Who Have Won Our Hearts

The Cry of the Crow

Dear Rebecca, Winter Is Here

Going to the Sun

The Grizzly Bear with the Golden Ears

Julie

Julie of the Wolves

The Missing 'Gator of Gumbo Limbo: An Ecological Mystery

The Moon of the Alligators

The Moon of the Bears

The Moon of the Chickarees

The Moon of the Deer

The Moon of the Fox Pups

The Moon of the Gray Wolves

The Moon of the Moles

The Moon of the Monarch Butterflies

The Moon of the Mountain Lions

The Moon of the Owls

The Moon of the Salamanders

The Moon of the Wild Pigs

The Moon of the Winter Bird

One Day in the Alpine Tundra

One Day in the Desert

One Day in the Prairie

One Day in the Tropical Rain Forest

One Day in the Woods

Shark Beneath the Reef

The Summer of the Falcon

The Talking Earth

Water Sky

Who Really Killed Cock Robin?: An Ecological Mystery

The Wounded Wolf

Jean Craighead George

THE FIRE BUG CONNECTION

AN ECOLOGICAL MYSTERY

HarperTrophy
A Division of HarperCollins*Publishers*

The Fire Bug Connection
An Ecological Mystery

Manufactured in the United Kingdom by HarperCollins Publishers Ltd. For information address HarperCollins Children's Books, a division of HarperCollins Publishers, 10 East 53rd Street, New York, NY 10022. Published simultaneously in Canada by HarperCollins Publishers, Ltd., Suite 2900, Hazelton Lanes, 55 Avenue Road, Toronto, Ontario M5R 3L2

Library of Congress Cataloging-in-Publication Data
George, Jean Craighead, date
The fire bug connection : an ecological mystery / Jean Craighead George
p. cm.
Summary: Twelve-year-old Maggie receives European fire bugs for her birthday, but when they fail to metamorphose and grow grossly large and explode instead, she uses scientific reasoning to determine the cause of their strange death.
ISBN 0-06-021490-2. — ISBN 0-06-021491-0 (lib. bdg.)
ISBN 0-06-440474-9 (pbk.)
[1. Insects—Fiction. 2. Science—Experiments—Fiction. 3. Ecology—Fiction. 4. Mystery and detective stories.] I. Title. II. Title: Fire bug connection.
PZ7.G2933Fi 1993 92-18005
[Fic]—dc20 CIP
AC

❖

First Harper Trophy edition, 1995.

To Sam

CONTENTS

THE FIRE BUG CONNECTION

1

BUGS, BATS, AND SPIDERS

Maggie leaned out the window. It was summer. She was back in the loft of the converted barn that stood in a dark forest in Maine. A wood pewee sang his predawn song. His plaintive serenade was followed by a long silence. Then over the purple mountains came the glorious aurora. A raven flew out of the light.

Maggie drew back. In all the years she had been coming to the research laboratory, she had never seen a raven. She was fascinated, then frightened. The great bird sped silently toward her. Its black iridescent feathers flashed green, then purple and blue. Its beak was big and thick; the eyes were polished ebony.

"When a raven flies at you, there will be a murder," she heard her grandmother telling her. She drew back from the window.

But he's not flying *at* me, she reasoned. He's flying *above* me. The raven suddenly back winged and dropped straight toward her. When it was so close Maggie could smell the birdy odor of its feathers, it swerved around the barn and sped away.

"Pooh," she said leaning out the window again. "I don't believe that stuff. Who would murder anyone here?"

But she could not put her grandmother's words out of her mind. This bothered her, for she knew she should not be frightened. She was a good naturalist. Creatures that alarmed other children—like bees and spiders and bats—were infinitely wonderful to Maggie.

Her love for them had begun when she was four years old. She had kept a long-legged house spider under a box and a click beetle in a jelly jar. When she placed the beetle on its back, it would arch, straighten its back, sail up into the air, and miraculously come down on all six feet and do it over and over again.

When she had been five years old, she had watched an ugly water nymph transform into a crystal-winged mayfly of great beauty. She had seen a praying mantis catch crickets with swift strikes of its front legs. At rest those legs made the mantis look as if it was praying, but when it went hunting, the front legs were switchblades.

Why, then, did she tremble at the sight of this raven, she asked herself? Her father had often told her that Grandmother's stories were largely superstitious and were not to be taken seriously. He, on the other hand, loved to teach her facts. When she had showed him her "bugs" one day, he had sat down beside her and held up her collecting jar so they could see them clearly.

"Bugs," he had said, "are one group of many groups of insects. They have beaks that pierce, not jaws. See the jaws? That's a beetle, not a bug. Now see the pointed mouth on the squash bug? That is a true bug. In addition to bugs," he had continued, "there are beetles, moths, butterflies, wasps, ants, bees, aphids, scale insects, as well as roaches, mantises, and grasshoppers, and forty-three others."

Then he had told her that her house spider was not an insect but an arachnid. It had eight legs; insects had six. The spider was related to the scorpions, daddy longlegs, ticks, and mites. Insects had three parts: a head, a thorax, and an abdomen. Arachnids had two parts: a head and an abdomen.

"But they are all Arthropoda," her father had said, "joint-legged animals. And we are Chordata, animals with backbones."

It did not matter to Maggie what her father called her six- and eight-legged friends—she liked them all. They did things. They burrowed, flew, changed body shapes, wove cocoons, ran backward, and did flips. Her mother had told her that ninety-nine point nine percent of the insects were harmless or downright beneficial, such as the bees that make honey, and encouraged her to collect and study them. Together they named and observed them.

Maggie had discovered at an early age that some of her insect friends were scary, and she loved these most of all. One was the bombardier beetle. It brewed enzymes and hydrogen peroxide in its abdomen and shot its enemies with a boiling-hot bullet of chemicals. Once Maggie had poked one of these iridescent blue-and-green beetles and been shot in the hand. The missile was 212 degrees F., and a blister arose to remind her not to tease a bombardier beetle again. But she went on collecting them—carefully.

No one thought this interest of Maggie's peculiar—at least not her family and her friends in the university town of Orono, Maine. She was the daughter of two scientists who were also professors at the university. Fred Mercer was a botanist and

Evelyn Mercer was a dendrologist: He studied plants, she studied soils.

Every summer the three spent their vacation at the Biological Research Station in the converted barn on the mountain in Maine. Maggie collected butterflies, beetles, and bugs. Her father counted plants to find which were endangered and why, and her mother studied the soil and the trees it nurtured. Her parents' findings were sent to scientists in the United Nations Environment Program. These people keep watch over the health of the Earth.

Maggie waited. The raven did not come back. She shook her head to rid it of her grandmother's haunting words and thought about something pleasant. Today she was twelve. She imagined her birthday would be like her other birthdays in Maine: the dawn, collecting, visiting, and a party at dinnertime. She smiled, then remembered a raven had flown at her.

". . . there will be a murder." Her grandmother's words would not go away. "Ridiculous," she said aloud. Convinced it was, she leaned on the sill to scan the sky. Presently a little brown bat flew in the window without touching her and alighted on a rafter.

"Hi," she said to the furry female bat. She had

named the bat Myotis, a scientific name like Tyrannosaurus or Stegosaurus. "Myotis" means "small brown bat" in Latin. Myotis squeaked and wrapped her webbed wings around a tiny baby bat near a nail on a rafter. The baby had been waiting all night for his mother. He suckled; then Myotis held him close and turned upside down so that she hung by her feet from the bottom of the rafter.

Another female bat hung nearby. She also had a pea-sized infant. She and her baby hung near a crack in the ceiling boards, so Maggie had named her Splinter. Maggie knew one bat from the other by their home spots on the ceiling, to which they were completely faithful. The two mothers took turns baby-sitting during the night, and with the return of Myotis both were now back.

Maggie always had newspaper on the floor to catch the rich bat droppings for the compost pile. She changed the newspaper and looked up at Myotis. The face of the little brown bat looked like an elf's. She had large pointed ears, tiny bright eyes, and a big cartoonlike smile. Myotis opened her huge mouth. Thirty-eight enamel teeth glistened. She was not showing off her teeth; she was sending out sounds so high-pitched Maggie could not hear them. They bounced off rafters, ceilings, bed, and table and told Myotis she was home.

When the bats went to sleep, Maggie sat on the windowsill to breathe in the pungent scent given off by the balsam fir tree that grew beside the lab. The tree was about as high as the roof and lustrous with dark-green needles. Its spreading branches formed a slender and symmetrical pyramid. Little blisters of resin on its smooth, gray bark and resin in its flat needles emitted a wild, fresh odor that filled the loft. Maggie breathed deeply.

At times she thought the tree knew her, although reason told her it could not. It had no brain or sensory organs. This morning, however, she felt this reasoning was wrong. The fir tree was whispering to her. Perhaps because of the raven. She reached out and broke off a small bough. The loft filled with the scent of northern trails and calling loons.

Wide awake now, she climbed down the loft ladder. She glanced at her parents under their puffy down blanket on the other side of the chimney. They were sleeping soundly.

Downstairs, the big one-room laboratory was dark. She could just make out the long tables under the windows. They were crowded with books, computers, journals, bottles of biological specimens, microscopes, and all the paraphernalia field scientists need. Each scientist who visited the lab was given workspace at the tables.

In the middle of the room was a large wood cookstove, and behind the stove was a pile of wood that reached from the floor almost to the ceiling. The woodpile was also a partition that walled off space with a cot and desk for visitors. Boxes of canned and dried foods and scientific supplies lined two walls. There was no running water at Bug Camp, and everyone liked to use the old pump outside and heat water on the cookstove.

The lab still held the good odors from the days when it had sheltered hay and horses. Maggie took a deep breath, then opened the front door, closed it quietly, and sat on the step.

As it grew lighter, she could see the abandoned field that stretched out before her, and beyond, the rugged mountains of Maine. Their ridges were jagged with the spires of spruce and fir trees.

Down the mountainside smoke began to rise from the Winters' house, and Maggie knew it was five A.M. The songs of the thrushes and vireos would soon fill the air.

Maggie loved this time of day. For many summers she had sat here in the twilight of morning, just as she was doing now, waiting for the birds to sing. Soon the spiders would finish their night work and the bees begin their day chores.

Maggie had been the only child in Bug Camp for many years, and she had invented her own amusements. Other scientists rarely brought their children to the lab, saying they thought there would not be enough for them to do in this isolated mountain spot. Maggie knew their kids better than that. Many of them were her friends, and she knew they loved to catch butterflies and grasshoppers just as she did. One friend collected tortoise beetles, which looked like tiny turtles. Some of the kids liked to fish, and most of them liked to make fairy gardens for their grandparents, uncles, and aunts. They put yellow-green moss and partridgeberries in large brandy glasses and covered them tightly with plastic or glass. The plants breathed in and out; made their own oxygen, carbon dioxide, and rain; bloomed and went to seed without further attention—fairy gardens were balanced ecosystems.

The truth was, Evelyn had said when Maggie asked her about it, with a few exceptions the parents did not want their children around the lab while they worked. One of the exceptions was coming today. Last night Maggie's father had told her that she wouldn't be the only child in camp for a week or so. Today James Waterford, the head of the forestry school at the university, was arriving. He was bringing not only the graduate student from the Czech Republic whom Maggie's mother had invited to the United States, but Mitch Waterford, his son.

Maggie knew Mitch well. He was ten years old and he was awful. He talked nonstop about computer games and the people he had beaten at Nintendo. He was also a pest. He had once charmed his way into several neighborhood houses and turned off the electricity to the invisible underground fences that kept their dogs at home. Feeling no electrical messages from the little transmitters under their chins, the dogs had run into the streets. Two had gotten into a snarling fight. The kids in the neighborhood had laughed and cheered the dogs on. The adults had grabbed garden hoses and sprayed neighbors and kids, as well as dogs, as they tried to stop the fight. Chaos had reigned.

Another time Mitch had jammed the school TV equipment with some device he had made. The New York Philharmonic orchestra was being aired on the television in the school auditorium. A program of Mozart suddenly became a program of humpback whale calls seemingly played by the orchestra. The kids in the audience had roared with laughter. The principal had summoned three electronics experts from the university, but as they came through the door, Mitch went off to the boys' room, and the problem suddenly cleared up.

Maggie sighed and wondered what was going to happen when Mitch got to Bug Camp. Of all the faculty kids, he was the one she least wanted to see.

2
THE RAVEN

Maggie jumped off the steps and ran through the meadow. The black-eyed Susans and yarrows took on their pert colors as the sun came up, and she forgot about Mitch and her grandmother-thoughts of ravens and murder.

A few moments later she was thinking about her spider, Araneus. She was one of the garden spiders that spin beautiful orb webs with spokes and spiraling latticework. Every morning Maggie watched her pull down her ragged, torn web, and every night she watched her weave a new one. Maggie wondered why she didn't mend her web and save herself all this trouble and work. Maybe she couldn't mend. To find out, Maggie had cut a large hole in Araneus's web last night, a hole so big a luna moth could have flown through it. Surely, Maggie thought, Araneus would not catch any food unless she darned that hole. Now she was on her way to find out if she had.

Araneus trifolium, a plump spider with greenish-gray abdomen and black and white spots on her back, was hiding when Maggie arrived. She was in a leaf tent she had made by pulling the edges of a leaf together with webbing. Maggie peeked at her. Araneus was in her parlor, but she had caught nothing last night. The huge hole was just as Maggie had left it.

"Araneus," she said, sitting down cross-legged before her, "you don't know how to mend. That's terrible." The spider came out of her tent and began reeling in her web.

"Perhaps," Maggie said to the busy lady, "I can teach you how to darn your holes tonight."

The web was hung from a cable of webbing that Araneus had stretched from a blueberry leaf to a milkweed plant. She never took the cable down at dawn, just the web. She would use the same cable over and over. While Maggie watched, the spider rolled up her web and carried the silvery ball to her hideout. There she ate it. Like all spiders, she had only so much silk to spin, and she did not waste it. But unlike any other spider, she tore down her entire web at dawn. By nightfall the silk would be ready to use again.

Araneus would sit quietly all day; then in the darkness of nightfall she would spin another web. Maggie had watched her construct her web one night and still marveled at what she had seen. Araneus had walked to the center of her cable and dropped into space, spinning as she fell. Her back legs pulled out the silk that made this plumb line. Like most spiders she had six hundred glands producing five different kinds of silk. She selected a strong dry silk to make the plumb line. When she came to rest on a twig she attached the thread, then climbed halfway up the plumb line. There she fastened, then spun out a loop and, holding it free of the plumb line and bushes, climbed to the cable, then ran along it until she found a spot to attach the webbing. She pulled the line taut and fastened it. This was the first spoke of her web. She then went down the spoke to the hub and spun out another loop, which she held loose. This time she went down the plumb line to a second cable she had stretched at the bottom of the web. She ran along it a short distance and attached it to the loop. Running back and forth to the hub, she carried threads and attached them first on one side and then on the other to keep the growing wheel spokes in balance.

When the spokes were done, she built a scaffolding by spiraling from one spoke to the next, outward from the hub. Then she ran up the plumb line and, standing on the scaffolding, spun a thick thread from one spoke to the next. She spiraled it inward. As she worked, she anointed each rung with a glue from special pipes in her spinnerets. The glue, so sticky a mouse would have trouble getting out of it, lay in messy globs on the thread.

Araneus then did an incredible thing. She pulled down on each rung and twanged it so that the sticky globs were spread out. The vibration distributed the glue evenly over the line.

The little spider moved in a spiral toward the center of her web, weaving and twanging. When she had built a perfect orb, she tore down the scaffolding and ate it. Then she went to the hub, attached a line, and, holding it loose, ran to her hideout. She turned around, made the line taut, and held it in both front feet. She was waiting for something to hit the web and jiggle the line. This was her own kind of telephone.

A jiggle usually meant some delicious insect had been trapped. But quite often it was a male spider, one third her size. He hid in his own leaf tent, occasionally daring to run out and jiggle the line to ask Araneus if she was ready to mate. It was wise to ask; she had already eaten two males who had not bothered to be so polite.

While Araneus ate her webbing this morning, Maggie wrote in her notebook, "Araneus can weave beautiful orbs of silver and crystal—but she cannot mend. I am going to try to teach her tonight."

The air was warmer when she finished her notes. Her great golden digger wasp would be getting up. Maggie put her pencil in her pocket and walked through foxtail grass and milkweed to the sandy bare spot in the meadow where Sphex lived. She lay down on her belly.

Several days ago Maggie had noticed the black wasp with the short golden body hairs and amber wings and had stopped to watch her. The wasp went into a hole in the ground, came out, flew away, and came back. After many hours Maggie realized that the wasp came back to her nest hole with the accuracy of a guided missile. She dropped out of the sky and hit it square on. During an interlude when the wasp was out hunting, Maggie fidgeted with the pine cones lying on the ground near the nest. They were nice ones, and she put several in her pocket for a fairy garden. When Sphex returned, she did not fly straight to her hole. Instead, she circled and wove as if she did not know where she was. Maggie wondered if the cones had been landmarks that steered the wasp home. She decided to find out.

Ten times she moved the cones, and ten times the wasp circled the objects before she landed. Ten times Maggie did not move the cones and ten times the wasp came straight home. If Maggie changed the cones while the wasp was in her nest, she would come out, hesitate, then take off and circle the cones as if memorizing them. If Maggie did not rearrange them, the wasp flew on a beeline to the field. "Sphex memorizes objects around her nest hole to guide her back to it," she wrote in her notebook.

This morning she had another plan. She was going to find out how far away from her nest the wasp memorized landmarks that led her home. Maggie gathered sticks from the edge of the forest and pushed them into the soil in a circle ten feet from the nest hole. She then sat down in the midst of the sticks and waited. If the wasp circled these, Maggie would know she memorized objects ten feet from her nest. The next day she would set up sticks twenty feet away from the nest. Eventually she would know how much the wasp saw and recognized as she came home.

As Maggie mused, Sphex suddenly dropped into her vertical hole with a grasshopper. Struggling with the large insect, which she had stunned with her stinger but had not killed, she finally disappeared down her hole. Maggie knew she would lay one egg in it. Next year when the egg hatched, the larva would dine on the grasshopper, which would still be fresh. A chemical in the great digger wasp's sting preserved it senseless, but alive.

Quark.

Maggie sat up. The voice was a new one at Bug Camp, but she knew from her birdcall cassette that it was the voice of a raven. Where was it? She scanned the mountainside. Only the smoke from the Winters' house moved through the trees.

She got nervously to her feet. Andy and Grace Winter lived all year around in the Maine wilderness and knew about everything wild. She would ask Andy about the ravens.

Quork. Another raven answered the first. This call was followed by a low knocking. Maggie took off running, at the same time watching the sky to make sure a raven was not flying at her. Snaking down a narrow footpath in the dark spruce and-fir forest, she arrived at the creek side. Here the path brightened. The birches and maples that grew along the waterway let in more sunlight than the evergreens. Under them grew a green carpet of ferns and wildflowers. She thought about gathering a few for a fairy garden.

Quork. Thoughts of murder replaced thoughts of flowers.

She sped around a bend in the trail and came out into the clearing where the Winters' house stood. She knocked on the door, and Grace opened it.

"Maggie Mercer," she said, and smiled. "Come in, come in!" She was a wiry woman with gray hair pulled straight back from her ruddy face like a cap. She wore L. L. Bean boots and a plaid skirt with a clean starched blouse.

The dark kitchen was illuminated by a window and flickering flames in the wood stove. The air smelled of hot maple syrup and fried bread. Maggie closed the door.

"Good morning, Mrs. Winter," she said, quite out of breath from running. "May I speak to Mr. Winter?"

"You sure can," she answered gesturing to the table by the window. "He's right here. And by the way, Maggie, don't you think it's about time you call us Grace and Andy? You're practically a grown-up now."

"Thank you," Maggie said. "I would like to do that."

Once Maggie's eyes had adjusted to the darkness, she could see Andy drinking his morning tea. His sleeves were rolled up and his white hair was combed neatly.

"Good morning," Maggie said. "I saw a raven this morning."

"Noble bird," he said. She stepped back. His deep voice always surprised her. It seemed to come from the bottom of some mountain well.

"It flew at me." She waited.

"That's nice."

"Grandmother says when a raven flies at you, there will be a murder."

"You know better than that, Maggie Mercer," Andy said, putting both hands around his tea mug and frowning at her.

"I know—but Grandmother knows a lot of things."

"She must be English or German," he replied. "Those Europeans thought ravens were murderers. Saw them on carcasses after their bloody wars and concluded that the ravens killed them or had something to do with it." He pulled up a chair for Maggie.

"Not the Native Americans," he went on. "They don't believe that."

"What do they believe?" Maggie asked, eager to

hear something better about ravens. Andy stirred his tea.

"My mother was a Wampanoag, one of the people who lived in New England before the Europeans came. They knew Raven well. He is never evil. He is the god who created the Earth, the moon, sun, stars, and people. He created the light by flinging glittering chips of mica into the heavens." Andy glanced out the window as if to check this out. "You call it the Milky Way." Maggie looked out the window, too.

"Raven is very powerful," Andy continued. "He created the menagerie—all the fish, birds, beasts, and the others—and then he created people." His dark eyes twinkled. "He created people for his own amusement. First he made us out of rock, but we were too durable, so he made us out of dust that would not last so long."

"That was sensible," said Grace, placing a cup of hot chocolate in front of Maggie.

"Nonetheless," Andy went on sternly, "you have to watch Raven. He can be a rascal."

"A rascal?" Maggie thought about the bird that had dived at her. "What did Raven do that was so rascally?"

"He created mosquitoes to plague us." Maggie laughed.

"And the Maine black flies," added Grace.

"Did your mother tell you this?" Maggie wanted to know.

"Yes, she and a Tlingit from the West Coast who came here to cut trees for the paper company. He also told me that the Tlingit and Eskimos say Raven turned the Earth over—from the darkness into the light. After Raven did that, he pulled the land out of the sea."

"Raven must be powerful," Maggie said thoughtfully, "if the people who live with him in the north and west and east all seem to think so."

"He is," Andy said, tilting his head so that the light cast deep shadows under his high cheekbones.

Maggie leaned forward. "Why haven't I seen a raven before this day?"

"They don't like people," he said. "Particularly white people. The Europeans thought they meant death. They shot them, poisoned them, trapped and burned them, until there were almost none left alive."

"But they don't anymore," Maggie said. "My dad said there are laws against killing ravens."

"Humph," said Andy getting to his feet. "They ARE making a comeback. Didn't use to be any around here. Now we have a pair nesting in the creek canyon." He walked to the back door and took down his plaid coat from a hook.

"Raven needs dark wilderness," he said. "When the forests were cut down for ship masts, firewood, and paper, Raven left. But the forests are no longer lumbered around here—trees not worth much—and Raven has returned. There are not many, but even one is a very good omen. He is good luck to me."

The corners of his broad lips turned up. "Grace and I are blessed to have Raven." He opened the door and looked out at the trees where the ravens lived.

"Maggie," he said, "I'm sorry I can't show you how wonderful Raven is. I have a load of firewood to deliver to Rumford. But this I know: It does not mean a murder will happen when a raven flies at you."

"Thank you," said Maggie, smiling. "I didn't think so."

"Grace can tell you about Raven," he went on. "We have a family of five in our valley—two oldsters and three youngsters. Their nest is in a white pine on the far side of the creek canyon. Grace talks to them. She calls them in, then chats with them." He looked over Maggie's head at his wife. "Don't you?"

"I don't know about that," Grace said in her slow

Down East way. "I know how to tell them I've got some chicken scraps or venison for them, but even a mouse knows when you're passing out food."

Maggie looked at Grace. She had always felt that Grace was a special person but now she saw she was an extraordinary one.

"So a raven flew at you, little Maggie?" Andy said, holding the door ajar. Maggie stepped closer to him.

"I heard his wings rustle and smelled his birdy scent, he was so near," Maggie whispered. "I was scared."

"Don't be," he said, taking the keys from his pocket. "Your grandmother's right; it's an omen, all right. But it's a good omen. Something new will be discovered."

"A new fish or butterfly?"

"Maybe a new idea," he said. "Something like that."

Maggie smiled. She already felt better about ravens.

Andy patted her head. "Why, Maggie," he said, "I'm getting hair as white as your own. Soon people won't be able to tell you from me." He smiled. "Except you'll still be the pretty one."

Maggie's hair was an unusual pale blond color

people thought was very beautiful, although she did not think so. To her it was straw. When she tried to curl her hair, it uncurled in a short time and fell straight to her shoulders. The best she could do with it was to put it under the visor cap that her parents insisted she wear to keep the ultraviolet light from harming her skin. But usually she forgot to wear the cap, so her hair stuck out like straw in a barn loft.

When Andy drove off, Maggie picked up her cup and carried it to the sink.

"Grace," she asked, "do you think you could teach me to call ravens?"

"I'd be glad to," Grace said, "as soon as I wash the dishes and sweep the floor." She took the kettle from the wood stove and filled the dishpan in the dry sink. Maggie picked up the broom.

When the chores were done, Grace went out the front door and put scraps of food on the porch, then she and Maggie took the trail to the creek. At the edge of the canyon they stopped under a balsam fir. A black bear had raked the bark with his long, powerful claws to say that the tree was his.

Grace took a crow call from her pocket. It was a short wooden spindle with a mouthpiece something like that of a clarinet. It had a small reed in it.

"My father made this," she said. "He made it to call crows, but when I do it right, I can call ravens."

Grace put the instrument to her mouth, took a deep breath, and blew. The sound she created was a high-pitched gargling sound, something like a huge baby bird asking to be fed.

"That's the raven yell," Grace said, lowering the instrument. "It means 'Come. Come. Food. Food'—I think." She winked at Maggie. "We'll see if it does. Keep your eyes and ears open."

A blue jay in the fir tree flew away. The forest creatures became very quiet. Even the evening grosbeaks stopped whispering. Maggie could hear the creek rushing down the mountain.

No raven came. Maggie looked at Grace. She had cupped her hands behind her ears. Maggie cupped her own hands behind her ears.

Quork. Softly, querulously, a raven gonged right above them.

Quork. Another answered from the creek. Maggie turned. A gorgeous black bird was sneaking toward them along the limbs, crossing from tree to tree. Silently he joined the bird in the fir. The bird in the fir crouched humbly before him and pulled in his neck. Feathers flattened on the creek bird's crown. Ear tufts shot up like horns. He looked terrifying. The bird in the fir lifted his head feathers, then the other bird flared his long tapered throat feathers and vibrated them like sabers. His flank feathers, like elegant pantaloons, drooped almost to his toes.

"That bird's talking with his feathers," said Grace. "He's saying he's a male, the poppa of his tribe. Isn't he grand?"

The raven emitted a sound like a stick hitting the pickets in a fence. He ended it with *thunk*. Then the birds flew away.

"That was the poppa saying to his child—'get home,'" Grace said.

"Really?"

"The young one thought I was a parent calling it to feed."

"You said that?"

"I think so. At least that's what the young one said by coming over to get the food."

Maggie stared at the tree where the ravens had sat. "The first one came when you called 'food'?"

"They have a language, too," Grace said.

"Do you know any other raven words?"

"Oh, I know lots of the sounds—" she said. "Quorks, queeks, quarks, yodels, soft melodious singsongs, thunks, pops; but I don't know what they mean, except that funny noise I just made—it means food, lots of it."

"But they didn't get any," Maggie said. "They'll never trust you again."

"Look at the front porch," she said, nodding toward it. Two ravens were stealing up the steps. One snatched a piece of chicken and hopped across the porch with it. The other covered a second piece of meat with its wings to hide it from lurking thieves, then picked it up.

"I put the food a far piece from us," Grace said. "They don't know you and probably wouldn't have come close. Aren't they handsome?"

Their blackness now looked like a metal armor, so solidly did it gleam. Their bright eyes burned with intelligence. Taking their food in their beaks, they lifted themselves into the air and flew into the dark forest.

"Where is their nest?" Maggie asked excitedly.

"I'll show you someday. Now, I've got to pick the blueberries before the little birds get them."

"And I've got to get home," Maggie said, looking at her watch. "Mom and Dad are expecting visitors today."

Grace picked up a basket and walked to the

trailhead with Maggie.

"Tell me about the raven you saw this morning, Maggie," Grace said.

"He flew at me. I know he did. As if he was telling me something."

"Was it a male?"

"I don't think so. If that bird with the horns was a male, then the one I saw was a female."

"Or a youngster," Grace said. "The youngsters are leaving the nest now to go exploring. When they get tired or scared, they come home."

"It might be the very youngster who came to your call," Maggie said with great excitement in her voice.

"Could be," mused Grace. "It's a bold one." She stopped walking. "Maggie, I don't know why that bird flew at you." She shifted her basket to the other hand. "I'm a Scot, you know, and my mother told me evil tales about ravens, like the one your grandmother told you. But, I've been living with them lately and I know they're not evil. They are rascals, all right." She laughed. "Andy's right about that."

"Speaking of rascals," Maggie said, "one is coming to Bug Camp today, and his name is Mitch Waterford."

"Maybe that's what the raven was warning you about—a rascal, not a murderer."

"In that case," said Maggie, smiling broadly, "Raven is right."

3
THE BIRTHDAY PRESENT

Mitch had arrived. He was sitting on the step of the lab, his brown hair standing straight up in a cowlick above his forehead. His slightly drooped eyes, with their heavy lashes, were scanning the terrain. He was already up to no good, Maggie thought, as she watched his glance shift from benches to axe to the holding cages for mammals and birds. He was wearing a purple vest. Enamel pins from various ski resorts practically covered the front of it, although Maggie was sure he didn't ski. She presumed he collected ski pins the way other kids collected baseball cards.

"Hi," he said as she came toward him. "What's to do in this dump?"

"Everything," she answered, and tried to step around him to open the door. Mitch did not move.

"Where do you play tennis?" he asked.

"In Rumford. The paper mill has a court." She tried to get by him again. "It's sixty miles from here."

"Where do you swim?"

"In the creek." She pointed down-mountain. "But you'd better be a good swimmer or you'll go over the falls." Once more she tried to get to the door. "Mitch," she said, "would you mind moving? I want to go in."

"Go on," he said, but did not move.

"It opens out," she replied. "You'll have to get up." Slowly, grudgingly, he arose. She pulled open the door and whisked inside.

"Happy birthday, Maggie," her mother called as she came in. She got up and gave Maggie a hug. Sitting at the folding table was a man in his mid-twenties.

"I want you to meet Mr. Capek Has," she said. "He's the graduate student from the Czech Republic I've been telling you about. Capek, this is my daughter, Maggie." The young man arose. He had a sharp nose, a pointed chin, and a haystack of brown hair.

"I am delighted to meet you, Maggie," he said, shaking her hand as if he meant what he had said. His accent was pleasant, and his smile captivating.

It exposed two rows of perfect teeth and elusive dimples low on his cheeks.

"I hear you are an entomologist," he said.

"Not really," she replied. "But I do like bugs."

"So do I." He smiled again, and Maggie could not help smiling with him. Capek, she knew, was going to be a nice addition to camp. He might even make up for Mitch.

"Since we are both entomologists," he went on, "I have brought to you a present that befits you and me. The present is from my country."

"Is the present some bugs?" she asked, teasing, but not at all believing what she had suggested.

"Yes," he said, and smiled. "You guessed it. Bugs. Wonderful, exciting bugs." He opened a large Styrofoam carrier and lifted from it a glass terrarium. "I had to file many forms and go through several inspections to bring the terrarium into the United States. Come to the window," he went on. "I want your first introduction to these little fellows to be just right." He put the terrarium on a table under the window so that the light fell on it. Maggie got down on her knees and peered in.

The bottom of the glass container was covered with sand and a few pretty stones that shone in the sunlight. Berries and seeds were scattered about. Climbing and flying, racing into the sun, red-dotted cloaks fluttering, was a host of attractive bugs. Their foreparts were black, their abdomens bright red. Each had black dots on its crimson back and black legs with joints of red. Their mouths were broad beaks.

"They *are* bugs, true bugs," she said, looking at the features that set them apart from all other insects, the sucking beaks and forewings that folded flat over the back. "They really are bugs!"

"Fire bugs," Capek answered. "*Pyrrhocoris apterus*. Happy birthday, my American entomological friend."

Maggie smiled at Capek. No one had ever before given her a present of bugs, or for that matter any insect. And they were pretty bugs. They reminded her of tiny Christmas tree ornaments.

"Thank you," she said, pushing back her pale-blond hair and looking up at Capek. "Thank you a whole lot.

"Mom," she called happily, "come see. Look what Capek gave me for my birthday."

"I do see," said her mother. She had noticed that Mitch had come in the back door and she was straining her neck to see what he was going to do. One of the dogs Mitch had set free during that notorious neighborhood incident had belonged to a friend of hers.

Maggie was asking Capek how to take care of the fire bugs as her mother crossed the room to the computer table where Mitch stood. She heard him say "modem" and whistle, then fall into a quiet conversation with her mother.

"They're easy to take care of," Capek said. "Just change the sand now and then, and feed them seeds and berries. Give them a few twigs of pine to climb on."

"How did you know I liked bugs?" Maggie asked, as a male fire bug, who was much smaller than the females, walked up to the top of a stone and flew like a burning meteor to a pine twig.

"Your mother mentioned your interests when she wrote accepting my application."

"How did you know it was my birthday?"

"I really didn't," Capek said. "Your mother told me after I arrived.

"As you know, I am going to help her study the effects of acid rain on a forest."

"She needs an entomologist?" Maggie asked. "She's a soil person."

"Acid rain weakens the trees, but your mother thinks insects and diseases actually kill them. I'm here to identify the insects."

"I wish we would just stop polluting the air with those stinky fumes from factories and cars that make all the trouble," Maggie said. "Mom says the sulfur dioxide from burning oil and coal combines with the rain and makes sulfuric acid—acid rain. It's deadly, you know."

"I know well. It is killing forests and lakes in my country," Capek said. "Did she also tell you that acid rain in the soil blocks the ability of the trees to take up the nutrients and minerals they need? She did some fine work on that."

"Isn't that what she got her award for?"

"Yes, it is," Capek answered. "A friend of mine checked her findings and found the forest trees of Europe and Asia where acid rain falls also suffer from lack of nutrients."

Maggie's parents often talked to her about their research just as other parents talk to their children about their work, but Maggie was aware of what acid rain did for another reason. She had helped her mother grow little spruce trees in a plot behind the lab. Some they watered with acid rainwater, some with pure well water. The trees watered with acid rainwater were yellow. They could not absorb the nutrients and were slowly starving. The others were healthy and green. But the yellow trees did not die until a bark beetle and a fungus attacked them.

Evelyn, Maggie's mother, thought the anti-air-pollution laws were not stringent enough by themselves to save the millions of acres of trees that were dying, but if the insects that killed them could be controlled, she thought, maybe the trees would survive. She had asked Capek to come to Maine to test this theory.

"Do fire bugs kill the weak trees?" Maggie asked.

"In my country they do, but for some mysterious reason there are no fire bugs in the New World."

"Then these are Pilgrims," Maggie said, looking into the terrarium. "The first fire bug settlers in America. Do I need to worry about them getting loose and becoming pests?"

"I have taken care of that," he said. "I have cleared them with the U.S. Department of Agriculture. Fire bugs are unusual. A friend of mine brought some to New England several years ago. They got loose, and that was the end of them. Fire bugs have an enemy in America. No one knows what it can be."

"Anyway," she said, "I'll be sure not to set them free. We have lots of pests in America that got away from experimenters—like the gypsy moth."

"Fire bugs are fun to raise," Capek said. "My father gave me some to raise when I was your age. I got many surprises." He smiled and, taking out a comb, flattened his unruly brown hair to his head. "And I hope so will you."

"They're pretty," observed Maggie. She was still on her knees staring at her birthday present. Capek got down beside her and watched two bugs that were merrily flashing like fire.

"Look," he said, enthusiastically scanning the terrarium. "You have about every stage of the fire bug's development here. I hadn't really noticed. There are eggs on the stem of that pine twig, and first-stage larvae feeding on the blueberries." He pointed. Maggie nodded.

"How many stages do they have?" she asked.

"Five," he answered. "The fifth molt is the show. That's when they metamorphose into adults. What a surprise you're in for." Capek smiled and looked more closely at the fire bugs.

"I see four fourth-stage larvae," he said. "Let's put them in a holding jar so you will be sure to see them change into adults."

Maggie went to the supply shelf in the visitors' room, glanced at Mitch, who was at a computer under Evelyn's supervision, and brought back two cylindrical glass holding jars. She lined them with newspaper so they could be easily cleaned. Capek put two red-and-black larvae and several juicy berries in each jar. He peered at the bugs.

"In a very few hours," he said, "you'll know why I brought *Pyrrhocoris apterus* all the way across the ocean to you." He smiled a dimple-accentuated smile.

Maggie took the holding jars and peered at her new friends. "They're big," she said.

"Yes; those two are females. The males are those little sparklers on that far twig."

"I can see red wings inside the coverings of the females' wing buds," Maggie told him.

"Ah," said Capek. "Maybe tonight they will shed for the last time, and"—he looked at her—"the dazzling metamorphosis." His hands opened and his fingers spread as if he himself had metamorphosed.

"Like a drab chrysalis to a beautiful butterfly?" Maggie asked.

"Like a fire bug," he answered. "And"—he put his finger to his lips—"I shan't tell you any more."

As Capek was getting from his knees to his feet, Jim Waterford came in the back door. He and

Mitch had been given one of the mountain tents behind the lab for their quarters at Bug Camp. Capek had the room behind the woodpile.

"Happy birthday, Maggie," the professor called, holding the door open for her father, Fred, who had an armload of kindling.

"Thank you," she said to the tall forester. He was wearing knickers, high socks, and ankle-high boots. Anyone, Maggie thought, would know at a glance that he was Mitch's father except that he wore a moustache and did not have a cowlick. They had the same egg-shaped heads and drooping eyes. The father also wore pins on his shirt, but his were pins from national forests.

"Happy birthday, Maggie," her father, said putting down the wood and giving her a hug.

"The birthday girl gets to pick the breakfast menu," Evelyn said, leaving Mitch and taking the folding table into the middle of the room. The table went up for meals, then down for space.

"Bacon, eggs, and oatmeal," Maggie said.

"Coming right up!" said her father.

"Jim," said Fred, when everyone but Mitch was seated at the table, "we have some plans for you and Capek to consider. We'd like to take a trip north to get your input on both Evelyn's project and mine. I'll tell you why I want to take this trip. A wood fern was once common around here," he said. "This field lab was as far south as it could grow. Anyplace on south of here was too hot for it. Now it is gone. I found it last spring thirty miles to the north, where it has retreated from the heat."

"Global warming?" Jim asked.

"Must be," Fred said. "Scientists working at the lab before us kept excellent records for ninety years." He pointed to the files along one wall. "The woodland deer mouse has retreated, too. Apparently it's too warm here for the fern and the mouse."

Maggie did not hear the rest of the conversation. She carried her fire bug terrarium to the loft and put it on her desk shelf. As she came back down for the holding jars, she noticed that Mitch was still at the computer, his face lit with its eerie white light. She had the feeling he had gone inside the contraption, and she hoped he wouldn't come out.

Suddenly a black thunderbolt shot past the window.

"Raven, Dad. A raven!" Maggie dashed to the door.

The breakfast eaters jumped to their feet and followed her.

"Where?" Fred asked, standing in the doorway. "I've never seen one here before."

The bird was gone.

"It folded its wings," Maggie said, pointing in the direction of the creek, "and dropped out of sight—*whoosh*—like a stone falling into the ocean."

"These northern ravens are uncanny," said Jim. "I helped an ornithologist livetrap and band songbirds for a study. The little birds screamed their distress cries when we lifted them out of the cages to band and let them go. Several days later we found the live traps sprung. Some had their doors torn off."

"Ravens?" asked Capek, as they returned to the table.

"That's what we thought," Jim said. "They lived in the forest. We never saw them after the little birds gave their alarm cry, but every morning another live trap would be rendered useless. Other strange things happened. The gas caps on our chain saws were unscrewed and had holes poked in them. The holes were the size of a raven's beak."

"A pair of ravens let the air out of my rubber boat when I was rafting the Allagash," Fred said. He chuckled. "I nearly went to the bottom before I discovered it."

"In Europe," said Capek, who had been listening with great interest, "we are not fond of ravens."

"In America," said Maggie, "some Native Americans believe Raven created the Earth, the sun, the moon, and the stars."

"I like that better," said Capek. "In my country they mean death."

Maggie looked from face to face, saw that no one took the European belief seriously, and, reassured, decided to ask Grace to take her to the ravens' nest.

She found Grace in the blueberry patch and, after helping her for several hours, walked with her along the creek trail and scrambled down the rocks to the water. Crossing the stream on a log Andy had felled, they pushed back interlocked spruce and fir limbs, and stopped beneath the raven's nest.

It was built of masses of sticks placed high in the top of a white pine tree. It was almost impossible to see from the ground unless you leaned against the trunk and peered up through the branches. Maggie did that.

Her spine tingled, and her heart raced. She had heard so much good and bad about the ravens that they, like the balsam fir by her window, seemed endowed with a special spirit.

"I see the youngsters," she whispered to Grace. "They're still in the nest."

"We're lucky," Grace whispered back. "They can fly short distances now. They come back to the nest to rest. Soon they'll be gone. Take a good look at them."

Maggie saw their great beaks and midnight-black feathers sticking out over the edge of the nest. She half closed her eyes, and daydreaming, saw Raven pull the Earth from night to day and the land from the sea. She saw the youngsters above her tearing doors off live traps and setting the mosquitoes loose on the earth. Then she tiptoed away.

"They *are* kind of magical," she said to Grace when they were scrambling back to the creek among white star grasses and ferns. "I'll bet they can even think."

"Oh, they can do that, all right," said Grace. "I tied a piece of bacon on a four-foot string then tied it to the limb of the maple by the back door. I wanted to see if the ravens could figure out how to get it."

"And did they?"

"Yes."

"Really? How could they possibly reach down four feet and get it?"

"I'll tell you how," Grace said, stopping and turning around to face Maggie. "One of them leaned down and pulled up as much string as he could reach."

"But he didn't get the bacon, did he?"

"No, he didn't. He pondered a moment and stepped on the string. Then he reached down and pulled up some more string. He stepped on that, did it again and finally got the bacon."

Maggie and Grace grinned with the delight of it.

"You're right," Maggie said. "That's thinking."

"Real good thinking," said Grace, striding off along the trail.

Maggie came back to the lab to find her mother cooking, the dinner table set, and a large present sitting at her place. She could read the card from the door. Huge red letters said "Love, Twelve-Year-Old, from Mom and Dad."

"Can I open it now?" Maggie cried.

"Not until dinner," Evelyn answered.

"That's hours away," Maggie complained.

"Go water the trees," Evelyn said, "and help your father put some new plants he found into his plant press. Skidoo. I'm cooking your favorite dish—lemon chicken."

Maggie finished her jobs and was back inside

with her father in less than an hour.

"Now?" she asked her parents.

"Oh, all right," Evelyn said, and Maggie opened the box.

"Boots!" she exclaimed. "Beautiful Gortex-and-leather mountain boots. How did you know I wanted them?"

"I don't know," said her father. "You never talked about them at all." He winked. Maggie laughed and hugged her parents, then sat down and put on her boots. She danced around the lab. Mitch never looked up from the computer. Maggie ran down the mountain to show her boots to Andy and Grace.

After a lively, noisy dinner, Evelyn took an ice cream cake from the freezer and everyone sang "Happy Birthday" to Maggie—everyone except Mitch. He had left the computer only long enough to eat his dinner, then took a piece of ice-cream cake to the computer later and ate it there.

After sunset Maggie went down to the meadow, determined to try to teach Araneus how to darn.

Carefully she made a hole in the silvery orb, then gently picked up a thread of webbing with tweezers and laid it across the hole. She laid several more strands of woof using threads from the bottom of the web. Next she laid down the warp. She didn't have to weave in and out as a person would in darning. The web threads stuck together. When she was satisfied that she had done the best she could, she stepped back and looked at her work. Not too good, she thought, but perhaps little Araneus would find it useful and be inspired to mend her web.

She went to her loft about nine o'clock. The adults were making plans for their trip north and Mitch was at another of the three computers.

Maggie stretched out on her bed and admired her very expensive mountain boots. She loved the boots, but she treasured more the parents who must have saved for a long time to buy them for her.

Smiling she looked up at the rafters. Myotis was baby-sitting the two tiny batlets. Gently, gently Maggie reached up and petted absent Splinter's little one. He was as soft as silk. He squeaked. Myotis crept over to him and took him under her wing.

"I won't harm him," Maggie said. "But you are a good nurse to check on him."

When Maggie was at last settled down and ready for bed, she kneeled before the fire bugs in the holding jars.

"When are you going to surprise me?" she whispered to them. "I'm eager to see what you do."

Quark.

Maggie jumped. The sound was so near, it frightened her. She listened. Hearing no more calls, she took courage, sneaked to the window, and turned on her flashlight. A silver eye shone in the darkness of the fir limbs. Just one eye, perceptive and undaunted.

She was glad she lived in America, where ravens did not mean death. Nevertheless, she jumped into bed and, pulling the blanket over her head, shivered deliciously.

4
THE RETURN OF THE RAVEN

The next morning the fire bugs had still not performed their spirited dance of change. Fat and round, they walked across the newspaper, chewing holes in it as they circled the jar. Maggie gave them fresh blueberries, then backed down the loft ladder to go and check Araneus's web.

To her surprise she found her mother awake and dressed, making oatmeal.

"Good morning, Maggie," she said.

"What are you doing up so early?" Maggie asked her.

"We're leaving for the north woods this morning."

"Am I supposed to go?" Maggie questioned.

"No," Evelyn replied, stuffing a log into the cookstove. "I'm sorry. I'd love to have you, but

Mitch doesn't want to go." Maggie wasn't sorry at all. She had her fire bugs, her spider, and her wasp. The only hitch was Mitch.

"It would be helpful if you stayed here with him," Evelyn said. "We'll be gone only a week."

Maggie groaned.

"Andy and Grace are coming to stay with you. Andy said he would cook venison stew and help you water the spruce trees."

Maggie brightened at the thought of having Andy and Grace for company. "Will the computers be working?" she asked her mother.

"Certainly," Evelyn said. "Why do you ask?"

"That will take care of Mitch, and the fire bugs will take care of me. We'll both have a good time." She walked to the steel bucket, dipped up a panful of water from the old farm well, and put it on the stove to boil for hot chocolate.

"Especially me," she went on with enthusiasm. "The fire bugs should have a surprise for me any moment now."

"You mean," called Capek from behind the woodpile, "they haven't changed yet? The four in the holding jars should have molted that fifth coat by now." He came out from behind the wood pulling on a turquoise-blue sweater.

"They did," said Maggie. "But nothing happened—no wings."

"No wings?" He looked puzzled. "They went through a fifth stage molt and are not adults?"

"Not yet."

"Perhaps I miscounted the molts," he said, frowning. Evelyn poured him a cup of coffee from the electric percolator. He accepted with a slight bow and went on: "I don't understand this." He looked very perplexed.

"Never mind," Maggie said. "The surprise should be even better for the wait."

"Seems as if the fire bugs still have surprises for me," he said, taking the doughnut Evelyn offered him. "Five molts, and yet you say they are not adults. I'd better have a look."

In a few moments Capek was back down from the loft.

"Very strange," he said. "They're grossly large; the biggest adolescent fire bugs I've ever seen."

"Then the show should be very soon," Maggie said. She picked up her flashlight and notebook. "Want to see an *Araneus trifolium*?"

"I certainly do," Capek said. "That's a delightful little spider." Capek knew precisely what spider Maggie was talking about. She had used its scientific name, eliminating any possible confusion that might come from a popular name.

Capek finished his doughnut and coffee, picked up his own flashlight, and followed Maggie into violet light of predawn. The wildflowers dropped dew on their boots as they walked. After a few minutes the call of the wood pewee announced the coming of the sunrise.

"The day's about to begin," Maggie whispered. She pointed to a young deer leaving the meadow for its day bed in the woods.

"The pewee has sung and the deer are going to sleep," she said. "That means 'good morning' in Maine."

The spider's web was not as Maggie had left it last night. A moth, wrapped in a broad band of silk, was hanging from Araneus's hideout. The battle between spider and moth had left a large rent in the upper part of the orb. Maggie's darning was unchanged, however. It stretched back and forth across the hole she had cut.

"See those silk strands across that lower hole?" she said to Capek, who nodded. "I made that patch to see if I could teach Araneus to mend her web."

"What an interesting idea," Capek said. "It never would have occurred to me to teach a spider to mend." He bent closer to Maggie's handiwork.

"Well, maybe you've never had to fix the knees in your blue jeans," she said. "Mending a web makes more sense than making a new one like Araneus does. I'm surprised spiders haven't learned this."

"Some have," he said. "But not very well."

Capek took out his magnifying glass and looked more closely.

"She didn't learn, did she?" he said.

"No," Maggie answered. "But she did use one of the threads I put down. See it? It's much thicker than the others. That means she walked across it and laid down another swatch of silk."

"Yes," Capek said. "This spider can't walk without leaving a thread."

"But she will never darn, will she?"

"She will never darn," said Capek. "She can't think."

"She can," insisted Maggie. "She used my web. Maybe she will pass that way of crossing a hole on to her kids and they will pass it on to their kids until, eons from now, there will be an Araneus who can mend a web."

"If you put it that way," he said thoughtfully. "Maybe she can learn."

Capek searched the leaves of the blueberry plant. "Where's the spider?" he asked.

"Under that leaf at the end of the cable." She pointed her light, and Capek bent down. The spider's eyes shone like tiny electric bulbs, but she did not run away.

"The light doesn't seem to bother her," he said.

"Neither does noise. She never runs when I come banging or singing through the weeds. But if I touch her web, oh, boy—watch."

Maggie picked a grass blade and touched it to the signal strand that led from the hub to Araneus. Araneus shot out of her leaf tent, ran a few steps, and stopped. She sensed the movement was not food.

"Now watch," said Maggie, taking out one of the moths she had caught at night when they came to her light. She threw it into the web below the darned hole.

This time Araneus came out of her tent, then ran down a spoke and across the darning without stopping. When she came to the moth, she turned around, spewed a wide band from her spinnerets, and, spinning the moth with her back feet, swathed it in silk. Then she bit it and ate.

"She does think," said Maggie. "She didn't wrap

the grass, did she?"

"Well," Capek said thoughtfully, "we need a lot more experiments to prove that is thinking. But," he said, shaking his head, "she does know the difference between a straw and a moth. And that in itself is marvelous."

"This whole Earth is marvelous," Maggie said. "There's a spider over here that makes a nursery web for her young to play on, and a wolf spider who lives in a hole. She carries her eggs up to the doorway and warms them in the sun so they'll grow. How does she know she should do that?"

Araneus was pulling down her web and rolling it into a ball when Maggie suggested they get back to breakfast.

"She's a good spider," she said to Capek. "She recycles."

As they came up the steep hill, the sun's pink light was falling on the tip of the tree beside the loft window.

"What's that tree?" Capek asked. "I don't know it. We don't have it in Europe."

"It's a balsam fir," Maggie replied.

"Very spiritual," he said walking up to it. "And," he added, breathing deeply, "as fresh as the Maine sunlight."

He broke off a twig and crushed it in his fingers. His nostrils filled with the piny scent. "Very nice," he said.

"Why does a tree need to smell so good?" Maggie asked.

Capek, taken aback, groped for an answer. "It must serve some survival purpose," he said, "but I really don't know. Perhaps someday we will. We are learning so much about plants."

"I think I know why it smells so good."

"You do?"

"Just so I can gather its needles and put them in pillows and sleep on them all winter when I'm far from the tree." She laughed to say she was teasing.

"You put these in pillows?" Capek said sniffing the twig more deeply.

"Everyone does. It's an industry in Maine and wherever the balsam fir grows. Would you like me to make you a pillow?"

"That would be very, very nice," Capek said. "I would prize such a gift."

Quork.

Capek looked around.

"Raven," Maggie said.

"Where?"

Maggie searched the trees in the direction from

which the sound had come, then cupped her hands behind her ears as Grace had done. She heard the rustle of feathers fade away.

"Gone," she said.

"Did I scare the bird?" Capek asked. "I am a stranger here. Ravens are wary and smart."

Maggie thought about that a moment. "It could be," she said, "but I really don't know. I think that bird is a young one. He keeps haunting me as if I have something he wants."

"That beautiful, glistening, blond hair," Capek said. "Ravens like beautiful shiny things."

Maggie ducked her chin into her shirt collar and blushed.

"That's silly," she said. To change the subject quickly, she told Capek about Grace and that she agreed with him that ravens were wary of strangers.

The members of Expedition North Woods, as Maggie now called it, were eating oatmeal, scrambled eggs, and bacon when she and Capek came in the door. Mitch, Maggie was grateful to see, was not up. She hoped she could eat and get out of the cabin to watch her wasp before he awoke.

Several hours later the North Woods Expedition said good-bye and walked down through the meadow to the laboratory vans parked on the road below. Maggie, with her notebook in hand, watched them go. As they reached the woods, Capek suddenly turned around and ran back.

"Maggie," he called, "would you check the fire bug adolescents once more? I'm really perplexed. They must be adults by now."

Maggie went inside and up the ladder to the loft.

"They're just the same," she called from the window.

She saw him shaking his head as he trotted down the trail to join the others.

Quork.

Maggie looked up. The raven was on the roof looking down at her. He seemed not at all afraid. In fact, he hopped closer.

"What do you want?" she asked.

He pumped his head up and down. Suddenly he flew toward her. Before she could throw up her arms to fend him off, he was rolling in the air and flying upside down.

"Grandmother," she said, looking at the fire bugs, "you may be right. My pets are being murdered in a strange and eerie way. They can't grow up."

5

PETER PANS

Maggie cleaned up the breakfast dishes before going outside to water her mother's spruce trees. When they were sopping in their respective waters, acid rainwater and pure well water, she picked up the axe and split wood for the stove. She was not very exuberant. She had a haunted feeling that her fire bugs were doomed—and it wasn't because of the raven, she said to herself. It really wasn't.

"Maggie!" Mitch was calling from the lab, and he was excited. She put down the axe and ran in the back door as he jumped from the loft ladder to the floor. His purple vest and red pants were a blur of streaming color. The ski resort pins sparkled brightly. Maggie thought a meteor had struck.

"Mitch!" she snapped. "What were you doing up there? That's my room."

"You've got bats in the loft," he said, and spun

around the lab until he found a butterfly net in a corner. He grabbed it and started up the ladder.

"Leave them alone, Mitch!" she shouted. "I want them there."

"You want them there?" He stopped on the second rung and stared at her. "You want them there?" he repeated. "Aren't you scared of them?"

"You know very well they're harmless."

"Yeah," he said, coming back down. "I know that, and I also know that they're the only mammal that flies, that one will eat two thousand insects a night, pollinate flowers, and rid people of mosquitoes. But I didn't know they were roommates for girls." He scratched his head. "How did you get them to come in your room?"

"Left the window open."

The boy stood quietly considering her words. After a moment a puckish smile appeared on his face. Briefly Maggie thought he looked rather nice. Then she remembered the dogfight in the streets of Orono and the TV concert at school.

"Mitch," she snapped, "did you rig anything in my room?"

"Nah," he said. "Couldn't think of anything." He walked to his father's workspace and sat down on the stool.

"You've got bugs that pop," he said.

"I what?"

"You've got bugs that pop. *Pfft*—explosion—dead." He grinned and looked around. "This place's terrific—bats, popping bugs, and"—he scrunched up his face—"I read your notes about the wasp. They got memories, huh?"

Ordinarily Maggie would have been furious at anyone going into her room, much less reading her notes, but she barely heard him.

"What bugs that went pop?" she said, knowing perfectly well what bugs.

"The little flame bugs," he said. "The ones with the fiery wings."

She climbed the ladder as swiftly as Araneus climbed her web; Mitch was right behind her.

Carefully picking up one of the holding jars, she looked at her friends.

"They *are* dead," she said. "And," she added slowly, "they're a lot bigger than they were last night."

Quork.

"What's that?"

"Raven." Maggie suddenly resented Mitch's invasion of her privacy. She leered at him.

"In Europe," she said, narrowing her eyes,

"ravens mean death." She held up the holding jar. "And murder."

"Murder?" Mitch said querulously. "Did someone murder the bugs?"

"Maybe you did," she said suspiciously. "What have you done to them?"

"Me?" he said. "Why would I do that?"

"Because you do all kinds of fiendish things, that's why!"

"Well, I didn't murder the little bugs," he said. Maggie looked into his eyes. He did not look away, and he did look innocent. Anyway, she finally said to herself, this was not Mitch's kind of prank. He was a hi-tech prankster.

"Well, then," she said, looking at the little insects, "we've got to find out who did commit the murder."

"Murder?" said Mitch. "Why do you keep calling it a murder?"

"It's a diabolical murder," she continued, "of the worst sort." She picked up one of the tiny creatures; it now looked like some kind of space alien with its feet up in the air.

"We have to find the killer," she said desperately. "Or there will be more murders." She spun around and glared at him. "A murderer is on the loose."

"Really?" Mitch looked terribly pleased.

"Yes, really," she answered. "And we've got to find him. These bugs came all the way from Eastern Europe for my birthday. They have been raised for generations by Capek and his father. Besides," she said, turning to Mitch, "the bugs were going to surprise me."

She put the two dead bugs in a glass vial for Capek to see when he came back and picked up the second holding jar. These larvae were also larger than they had been a few hours ago. She looked more closely. Two small coats lay on the paper. Like the dead fire bugs, these had molted and stepped out of their fourth-stage coats and gone into a fifth larval stage. They should be adults with wings. They were not.

"Are they going to go pop?" Mitch asked, peering over her shoulder.

"I don't know," Maggie said, looking at them carefully. They stopped chewing the paper on the bottom of the holding jar and stared back at her.

"Something's wrong," she said. "They can't grow up."

"Like Peter Pan?"

"Yes, like Peter Pan," she answered distractedly.

"Neat," he said.

"It's horrible," she replied. "They'll never have children."

"Must be something in the environment," said Mitch. "It always is—acid rain, maybe."

"Maybe," said Maggie, now studying the fire bugs in the terrarium. Several were in the fourth stage and about to metamorphose. Gently she picked them up and put them in the empty holding jar.

"Ugly," said Mitch. "Let me see 'em. I love ugly things."

"They're not ugly," Maggie snapped. "Look at their ruby backs and fiery leg joints. They're cute. Even their antennae are perky and shiny."

"How do you know they won't grow up?" Mitch asked. "Maybe tomorrow they will."

"Well, the others popped and died, didn't they?" But Mitch was right. She really didn't know. Sitting down on her cot, she stared at the fire bugs in the terrarium. One adolescent in the fourth larval stage was in the terrarium, sitting quietly on a pine needle. She was about to pick it up, but as suddenly as if it had been touched by a laser beam, the fire bug lit up, and her chitin coat began to split.

"Mitch," she whispered. "The metamorphosis. Here comes the surprise."

Mitch got down on his knees to be at eye level.

"Which one's surprising us?" he asked, and Maggie pointed her out.

As the coat fell away, the nubbin wings moved. The creature reared up on its two back feet, and like the flames of a roaring fire, the wings grew. They trembled and fluttered until glassy black dots appeared in the bright red casing. The wings trembled until they reached their full length, then they fell flat against the little back. The adult female fire bug rested. Presently she flew to a stone.

"That was two surprises," said Maggie excitedly. "One fire bug show, and one healthy adult."

"Anyone home?" Grace Winter called from below.

"We're up here, Grace," Maggie answered. "Come on up and see my fire bugs."

"Come on down," she answered. "I've got soup for you."

Mitch was down the ladder before Maggie could replace the lid on the terrarium. He hit the floor, spun around, and climbed back up two rungs.

"It's the hole in the ozone layer!" he yelled. "It's got to be. It's murder and the ozone layer did it." He jumped from the second rung to the floor.

"Oh, brother," said Maggie, rolling her eyes.

"Hello," said Grace. "You must be Mitch." She shook his hand. "I'm Grace Winter. My husband's bringing in a bag of potatoes. Run out and introduce yourself. It's been a long time since he's seen such a fine boy as you."

"He's not fine," said Maggie as she came down the ladder. "Beware of him. I know."

Mitch stuck out his tongue at her and grinned. He started toward the door, then turned back to Maggie.

"I *know* it's the hole in the ozone layer," he said. "It's gotten much bigger. It's over Europe, the Antarctic, and now North America—right over Maine for that matter. It's letting in too much ultraviolet radiation. That causes cancer. Cells grow out of control. The cells of the fire bugs grew until they popped. Cancer; what else?"

"Goodness," said Grace Winter. "What are you talking about?" She opened the stove firebox and added some wood.

"Peter Pans," Mitch answered. "Maggie has a bunch of Peter Pans upstairs. They won't grow up."

Quork. The noise came from the balsam fir.

Quark. This noise came from from the yellow birches.

"RRRRRRRRRR." That noise was like a stick

being run along a picket fence.

Maggie ran to the window.

"The ravens, the ravens! Grace, you've brought the ravens! I knew you would." She ran out the door into the bright noon light. Two ravens flew away. A third hopped closer to her. Maggie looked for the parents, who might attack her if she got too close to their youngster, saw none, and walked toward the bird.

"Was Grandmother right?" she asked the raven. "There has been a murder in the loft."

The bird backed up as Maggie stepped toward it. Suddenly he took off and skimmed over her. He came so close she could see on his head a few last straggly pinfeathers, the feathers that adorned him as a baby. Her raven, she now knew, was a young bird, no doubt from the nest in the creek canyon. She was thrilled that he seemed to recognize her, but she was also wary. She did not know what he had in mind—but that he did have *something* on his mind was now very clear to her.

6
SUSPECTS

For the next three days Maggie and Mitch, because she couldn't stop him and because, in fact, she was beginning to enjoy his company, kept notes on the young fire bugs in the holding jars. None of them grew up. Seven became sixth-stage larvae and puffed up and popped.

"They always pop when the ravens call," Mitch remarked. "Raven did it."

"Come on, Mitch," Maggie said, opening the notebook. "Here are two that popped before the sun came up and the ravens weren't even around." Mitch looked at the notes and scratched his head.

"Then it's the hole in the ozone."

"You're not thinking, Mitch," Maggie scolded. "They're indoors out of the sun—how can the ultraviolet rays affect them? And the murderer isn't even acid rain. The fire bugs don't get rained on, either."

"But they eat berries that got rained on," he said.

"I hadn't thought of that," she said, turning quickly to the jars. "Something in the food, maybe?"

While Maggie was pondering this, Mitch looked up to see the bats. They were sleeping peacefully although he and Maggie were talking and moving around. Perhaps the bats liked them.

Quork.

"It's Raven," he said. "Raven did it. Even Andy told me Raven's a rascal."

"Mitch," Maggie said in exasperation, "get lost. I'm trying to think."

"Okay for you. I just think I will," he said, and backed down the ladder.

Maggie was sorry she had run him off. He would go back to the computers and she probably wouldn't see him again for the rest of his visit. That would be too bad. He had been a real help with the solitary wasp. She had taken him out to the sandy hillside to prove to him that the wasp memorized the objects around her nest. Intrigued, he had gotten down on his belly and watched as Maggie took away pine cones and rearranged stones. The wasp never failed to circle new objects when she arrived or departed, and she never failed to hit the hole directly if the objects remained in place.

Maggie heard the door slam as Mitch went off in a pout. She must make amends, and she thought she knew how. She leaned out the window.

"Mitch," she called. "It's time to check the great golden digger wasp." Mitch walked on.

"Sphex will soon finish her nest, and we won't see her again." That did it; Mitch turned around. Maggie ran down the ladder and caught up with him at the nest site. They quietly got down on their bellies.

"How do you know it's the same wasp every time?" Mitch asked.

"Because it's a solitary wasp, *Sphex ichneumoneus*, the great golden digger wasp. Only one attends the nest."

"How do you know?"

"I know a solitary wasp like you know computer games."

"But you don't really know," he said. "You can't tell one golden digger wasp from another. They may be taking turns." Mitch watched the wasp arrive on a beeline.

"Look her up in the insect field guide. You'll see."

"That doesn't prove anything," he said, getting to his knees. "I'm going to mark her and find out."

"How?" She asked, intrigued.

"Next time she sticks her head out of the hole, I'll daub her with poster paint. Then we'll be able to recognize her and know for sure."

Maggie sat back, her legs out straight, her hands propped behind her as Mitch ran up the hill to the lab. What a great idea, she said to herself. Marking the wasp would make it a recognizable individual, and I can learn lots of things from an individual—where it goes, who its friends are, where it sleeps.

Mitch returned with a bottle of white poster paint and an artist's long-handled paintbrush used for dusting insects and other delicate specimens. He got back on his belly. The wasp came out almost instantly and too fast. He dabbed and missed. She came out too fast the second time and he missed again.

"I'll change the pine cones," Maggie said, moving a cone and adding a rock. "That makes her stop and look around. It'll slow her down."

"Yeah, yeah," said Mitch, wiggling closer and bracing his right hand with his left. The wasp emerged, hesitated, and looked for her guideposts. As she did so, Mitch put a dab on her thorax. She flew up and circled her hole twice, then shot out over the meadow. The two hunched down to await her return.

"Maggie!" Grace Winter called. "I need some help."

"I'll be back," she said to Mitch. "Here's the notebook. Write down everything you see—and the time and date."

She ran all the way to the lab and helped Grace by carrying the potato peelings to the compost pile, shaking down the stove, and taking out the ashes. Then she helped Andy peel carrots and onions for venison stew. When the chores were done, she went to the loft to tend the fire bugs.

She took out the soiled and chewed paper from the rearing jars and put down fresh, clean paper. She washed out the tiny drinking dish and refilled it with water.

"It might be the water that killed the little bugs," she said to herself. "Our well water must be different from the water Capek had." She started down the ladder to sterilize a bottle of water with a chlorine pill, but Mitch was coming up at the same time.

"You're right," he said when they met. "There's only one wasp."

"I'm glad that's settled," she said, and climbed back to the loft with him.

"Mitch, I think it's the water that's making them

Peter Pans," she said. "That's the only thing that is different from their home in Czechoslovakia."

"I think it's the ozone hole. It's letting the ultraviolet rays mess up Raven's brain so that he is putting a curse on your little pets." He laughed and turned a somersault on her bed.

"Stop kidding," she said. "These little bugs are a present to me, and I'm letting them die. Please help, Mitch. You're smart. You can think."

"Well, it's not the water," he said, "or they all would die. The ones in the terrarium become adults, and they drink the same water."

"That's right," Maggie said, scratching her head and looking from the terrarium to the holding jars.

A squeak sounded above their heads, and Myotis swirled quietly around them. As gracefully as smoke from an autumn bonfire, she went out the window and into the late-morning light.

"It's early for her to go hunting," Maggie said. "She's never out in the day."

"Neat, ugly critter," Mitch remarked with a grin; and then, before Maggie could get angry at him, he added, "I did something else."

"What?" Maggie's voice was anxious.

"I made three more nest holes to see if the wasp knew which one was the real hole."

"Did she?"

"She circled and circled then suddenly—zoom—she hit the right hole. No problem."

"What does that mean, I wonder?" said Maggie.

"That she sees *and* smells," he answered with finality. "She couldn't tell which was which until she was close enough to smell her larvae or something. Then bingo, in she went."

He took a breath, then said, "I did something else."

"Now what?"

"I took away all the stones and cones and brushed the ground until it was smooth and the nest hole was covered up."

"And?"

"She came home, circled and circled, couldn't find her nest, and did something real smart."

"What?"

"She landed and hunted for it on foot."

"Did she find it?"

"Back and forth she went, and then suddenly she started digging, not where I thought the nest was, but another place. She threw out sand grains with her front feet and went in. She found it."

"She can think?" asked Maggie cautiously. "It seems to me she figured out she had to walk, not fly, to find a buried hole."

"Seems so," said Mitch.

"We've got to show Capek this."

"I did something else."

"Oh, Mitch, now what?"

"I took away that egg case Araneus made yesterday. I hid it."

"Mitch, no!" Maggie was horrified. "That's terrible. The eggs are her children. You're torturing her."

"I gave her a copy I carved out of a cork."

Maggie stared at him.

"What did she do?" she asked, reluctantly but eagerly.

"She took it."

"She took it?"

"Yes, she's smart enough to do geometry, but she doesn't know an egg case from a cork."

Maggie sat down.

"Poor spider" was all she could think to say. Then she added, "Poor spider, to have met up with Mitch Waterford." She looked at him. "Now that you know she doesn't know her egg case from a cork, please return it to her. Please."

"Okay," he said.

Quork!

Maggie dropped to her knees before the holding jars. The Peter Pans went on chewing away at the paper and the berries. None of them popped.

"See?" said Maggie.

"I see," Mitch said. "But I remember one popping when the ravens called."

"One is not enough," she said. "The thing to do now is make a note of when the ravens call and *then* check the fire bugs."

"This is getting too complicated," he answered. "Let's eat."

Myotis returned. When she had fed her baby and turned upside down, Maggie could see a caddis fly clinging to the corner of her mouth.

"No wonder you went out in the daylight," she said to the bat. "There's been a hatch. That means billions and billions of caddis flies over the creek. Now how did you know that?" she asked.

"I guess she heard them," Mitch said. "She has awesome ears. I'll bet she can hear a solar wind."

That evening was warm, so Maggie suggested they eat outdoors. Last night before sunset the ravens had come to the balsam fir, and Grace had fed them leftovers. She hoped they would come again tonight.

"Maggie," Grace said, as she carried the folding

table to the door, "there's a letter from your mother on her worktable. Andy went to town this morning for the groceries and mail and I forgot to give it to you. I'm sorry."

Maggie tore open the letter, read a glowing description of the campsite in Baxter State Park, and then read aloud:

"We may not come back as soon as we had thought. I have found severe yellowing of the older needles of the red spruce trees up here. Acid rain has come to Maine with a vengeance."

Maggie read louder.

"Will you tell Mitch to print out an article that appeared in a recent issue of News Magazine*? It's called 'The Benefits of Dirty Air' and is about sulfate aerosols that pollute. Tell him to dial the university and get NEWS. It will be on that program. He can fax the article to this number: 207–555–9292. It's a pizza parlor. How about that?*

"I love you very much and wish I could be there to see the fire bug display.

Mom."

Mitch turned on a computer, dialed the university, and waited. The screen filled with a window of queries. He typed answers.

"Found it," he said. Presently the laser printer whirred and a page rolled out. Mitch picked it up.

"Wow," he said. "Some guys have found that the sulfate aerosols from burning oil and coal may help ward off global warming. The article says these dirty aerosols reflect sunshine and seed clouds. Clouds bounce sunlight back to space. This makes for a cooler planet."

"In other words," said Maggie, "they are saying that coal and oil pollution has not warmed the globe as much as we thought."

"That's what they're saying."

"The aerosols are still bad," said Maggie. "They make acid rain. Acid rain kills forests and life in freshwater lakes."

Andy came in the door. "Where's the folding table?" he called. "I've got the venison stew bubbling on the coals out there. It's time to eat."

Maggie carried out the table and Grace brought the bowls and flatware. The scent of stew and smoke brought Mitch on the run.

They had just started eating when two ravens flew silently into the balsam fir and took their perch. They raised their crest feathers and posed, heads slightly up, like a king and a queen.

"Those are the adults," Andy observed. "The youngsters should be here soon." They waited quietly for the young ravens to join the parents, but they did not appear.

Andy walked a distance from the table and scraped his bowl. He glanced up at the two regal birds.

"No kids tonight?" he asked. They gargled and quorked as if they were answering him. Andy thought they were discussing whether or not the food was a trap. "Might be a coyote hiding behind a clump of grass ready to jump on them," he said. "They're very cautious. Ravens don't make mistakes."

"Where are their kids?" Maggie asked.

"Looks like the good life is over for them," Andy said. "Raven parents run their youngsters into the next county shortly after they're out of the nest. They don't tolerate them anymore."

"That's cruel," Maggie said. "They're still so young. The one I saw still had its baby feathers."

"Depends on who you are," said Andy, "a parent or kid. Winter's coming and there's only so much raven food. The kids have to fend for themselves."

"Well, I'm a kid, and I'm going to feed the kids," she said. She picked up her bowl and went in search of the young ravens. She thought she had heard that baby hunger cry in the forest behind the lab.

She circled the tent where Mitch and his father slept, then her mother's plot of trees, and entered the gloomy, dense forest. At a short distance, she saw three frightened young ravens hunched on the dead limbs of a balsam fir. They sat perfectly still, their thoughtful eyes upon her.

"Here," she said, scraping her bowl. "This is for you." The food lay on green moss beside purple star grass and toadstools. The birds eyed her fearfully. She backed away.

Quork.

Maggie looked at her watch: 5:35 P.M. Even though she didn't really believe Mitch's theory could be true, she would check the fire bugs to see if any had popped and died.

As she went back down the trail toward the lab, the two adult ravens sped past her like black missiles and alighted on a limb above the venison. The young ravens took off in silence. The parents, after waiting again to see if an enemy would challenge them, dropped to the ground and ate.

"They're awfully young to be treated so badly," Maggie said, searching the dark forest for the raven children. The shadows of night tangled with black-and-white birch trunks, dark needles, and limbs, and she could see no farther than ten feet ahead.

So she listened. A porcupine swished his quills nearby, but she could not see him. Katydids sang, a woodpecker screamed, and the balsam firs gave off their fresh scent. But she did not hear the young ravens, who were alone and unfed in the forest.

Returning to the lab to put a bucket of water on the stove for dishwashing, she noticed that Mitch was not at the computer, although it was turned on. Wherever he was, he would be here soon, she said to herself, for Grace had opened the oven door and was reaching for a golden pie.

"Blueberry," Maggie said, when the incredible odor of wild Maine berries reached her nose.

"Mitch," she called, "Grace has made a blueberry pie. Come on." He did not answer. She decided he was in the loft and went to the ladder. She heard his feet shuffle.

"Blueberry pie, Mitch," she called. "And Mitch, before you come down, look at the fire bugs. A raven quorked at 5:35 P.M. See if there's been another murder."

No answer. She shrugged and followed the scent of blueberries out the door. She and Andy waited while Grace returned to the lab for a knife and a pie lifter. Smiling with anticipated pleasure, they watched her divide her masterpiece.

"Where's Mitch?" Maggie finally asked when the slices were distributed.

"He's back at the computer," Grace answered.

"Lost," Maggie said. She took a bite of pie, closed her eyes and *ummmmed*.

Footsteps sounded inside the lab, and the purple-and-red meteor leaped out the door and took his place at the table.

"Yumm," he said after tasting the pie. "I'll bet my dad's not eating like this. What great cooks you are, Andy and Grace. Just great." He toasted them with a bite of pie and did not speak again until his share was finished.

"It's not the ravens," he said, scraping his plate. "I heard one quork at 5:35 P.M., so I checked, and nothing popped and nothing died."

"Good," Maggie said. "Now we can look for something else."

"And I know what it is," said Mitch.

"What?"

"Global warming," he answered. He grinned.

"I'll prove it. This time I have the research to prove it." Maggie sighed.

"You kids are too much for me," Andy said, getting up from the table. "Half the time I don't know what you're talking about. Let's clean up and go catch a fish for breakfast. Or *do* you know what I'm saying?"

"I sure do," said Mitch, getting to his feet.

"And I do, too," said Maggie. She began to clear the table. "Let's wash these up and go."

7
ON-LINE ACCESS

The next morning the Winters went home to water their garden while Maggie and Mitch washed and dried the breakfast dishes.

"What makes you think it's the global warming?" Maggie asked as she held up a cup to see if she had gotten it clean. "There may not be such a thing. You just read yesterday that sulfate aerosols might offset the heating of the planet by making clouds."

"Well," Mitch said, picking up a dish and drying it, "those scientists in the article are not keeping weather records. Let me tell you something. The Earth's atmosphere *is* warming. I just read on the lab's on-line access that weather records show that global warming over land has been about one degree Fahrenheit in the past century. That's a lot."

"But what's it got to do with our fire bugs?"

"I'll show you," he said, throwing down the dish

towel and going over to a computer. "Come here." Maggie took her hands out of the soapy water and dried them on her pants as she followed Mitch. He turned on the computer. The screen lit up, the machine made some boings and whirs, and then there was a blur, half a message, and a chart.

"What are you doing?" Maggie asked.

"The lab has some pretty fancy telecommunications and gateways," Mitch said, hitting keys and waiting. "But your mom didn't tell me about this third computer and BIOLIN. I dial the university computer and it gets me BIOLIN. BIOLIN got me into the abstracts and full texts of all the biological papers and journals. Look at this."

Maggie leaned over his shoulder. "Aug. 15 Proceedings of the National Academy of Science." She knew about the National Academy of Science. Her parents talked about this prestigious group of scientists quite often.

"You mean to say that the National Academy of Science figured out that global warming killed our fire bugs?"

"Sort of," Mitch said. An article appeared on the screen. "This article," he said, "says that grasshoppers split and shed their coats when it gets too hot. That's what our fire bugs are doing. They are splitting their coats and shedding them. They're shedding because they're too hot—global warming."

Maggie sat down and read the article. Scientists in California had found that all insects could shed their coats to adapt to the local environment, particularly heat.

"But the article doesn't mention global warming, Mitch," she said.

"Doesn't have to. Use your head. It's hot, they shed. That's what our bugs are doing."

"Ours are not only shedding," she told him. "They're not growing up. They don't mature and have young. That's the problem, and the article didn't say anything about that."

She went back to the dishes, thinking about the fire bugs and heat. If it was too hot for them in the loft, why had one successfully metamorphosed?

Mitch concentrated on the computer. "Listen, to this, Maggie," he called. "This is from *Science* volume two thirty-four: 'The snow mantle in the Northern Hemisphere is turning to slush. The sea ice near Greenland is thinning. Alaskan snow melted two weeks earlier in the nineteen eighties than the nineteen forties and Ontario's average annual temperature climbed more than three and a half degrees Fahrenheit from the late sixties to the mid-eighties.'"

"And you think that is enough to make the fire bugs shed?"

"Yes."

"And not have babies—and die?"

"Yes."

Maggie carried the dishwater out to the filtering pit, and dumped it. Standing quietly at the edge of the forest, she listened for the young ravens. She did not hear one baby call, although she waited a long time before going back to the lab.

"They die," said Mitch as soon as he heard her return, "because they can't move north. They're stuck in that glass terrarium in your loft. Listen to this journal from the University of Michigan: "'A mouse no longer lives in a county of Michigan where it has for the eighty years scientists were keeping records.'" He turned to Maggie. "The journal goes on to say that particular species of mouse requires cold weather to survive. It's gone north. They found it in Canada. Global warming."

"Oh, Mitch," Maggie said, picking up the broom. "I don't see what that's got to do with our fire bugs."

He would not be discouraged. "'The fine-scale dace,'" he read, "'a little minnow that thrives only in cold water, has disappeared from the same place in Michigan. Now it lives far to the north. And some animals that thrive in warm weather have pushed north, too. The Virginia possum, the armadillos, cardinals, mockingbirds—a lot of things.'"

"And some plants," Maggie said. "That's why Daddy's up north with your dad. The atmosphere *is* warming, I agree with you. But Mitch, the mice have mice and the fish have fish, but the fire bugs are not having fire bugs. That's the problem."

Maggie folded up the table and put it away before going off to see Araneus and the wasp. When she returned many hours later, Mitch was where she had left him, poking into all manner of programs on the computer that she knew nothing about.

She climbed to her loft and looked at her little charges from Czech. All the youngsters in the holding jars were Peter Pans. They were pretty; they frisked and ran over the paper. But they would not grow up. She sat down and stared at the jars—thinking, thinking. Who was doing this? Who was murdering her fire bugs in such a bizarre manner?

That evening she returned to the loft to ponder the fire bugs again. Myotis dropped from the rafter near the nail and circled her head. Maggie watched her as best she could; watching her fly was like keeping track of a tumbling aerialist. Even a glimpse of her told Maggie the little bat was thin. Maybe she wasn't getting enough food. Her baby was so big he needed a lot of milk. In fact, she realized, Myotis and Splinter were no longer taking turns baby-sitting. They both went foraging now and left their babies behind. They must trust me, she thought, and hoped it was true.

Maggie took a moth out of the jar of moths she collected for Araneus and held it in her fingers. The moth fluttered its wings; Myotis heard it and alit on Maggie's hand. She could feel the little feet and cool webbed wings.

Maggie touched her dense soft fur and smiled. Myotis swallowed the moth, then took off and flew around her head before flying out the window to join the insect hunters of Maine's nighttime skies.

The babies hung upside down, their eyes closed, their little wings collapsed like folded umbrellas. Maggie blinked. She thought she saw a yellow spot on one of the baby's backs just above the tail.

"Mitch!" Maggie shouted. "Mitch!"

His head came over the loft floor. "You saw it, huh?" he said sheepishly. He hesitated and then came on up.

"Why did you paint them?" she asked. "What

have you done to my beautiful bats?"

"I color marked Myotis and her friend," he said. He squatted before the fire bugs, pretending that he was very interested in them. When Maggie said nothing, he went on.

"I wanted to find out if they knew their own babies." He glanced at Maggie to see how she was taking this. She did not look mad, so he continued. "I daubed Myotis with yellow poster paint and Splinter with white." Maggie still said nothing, so he continued, this time with more excitement in his voice.

"Then," he said, looking at the rafters, "I marked each baby the same color as its mom." Maggie was tapping her fingers on the edge of her bed. He talked more quickly, sensing her rising exasperation. "I wanted to find out if they knew their own babies. Some scientists don't think they do."

Maggie stared up at the tiny bats hanging on the rafter and ceiling board. She squeaked to them and they moved a step or two toward her. Now she could see a yellow spot on the lower back of one, a white spot on the other. She got up on her bed and took down the baby bat with the yellow spot. Some of the paint flaked off. It would not be there very long. Mitch's experiment could only last a few days and would do no harm, so she did not wipe off the paint.

"Well, what did you find out?" she asked. She wasn't mad at all. "Do they know their babies?" She wanted to know too.

"I won't know until they come back in the morning," he said. Maggie stroked the furry infant. He opened his huge mouth ringed with tiny teeth and squeaked a high, thin cry. The little eyes flashed like silver pinpoints.

"I wanted to switch the babies as soon as the moms left."

"Mitch!"

"But you came back too soon."

"Well," she said, "we can do it now. Whose baby do I have?"

"Yellow belongs to Myotis."

He put a stool under the baby roost and stood on it. Gently he moved Splinter's baby to the spot near the nail where Myotis hung her batlet.

"Let me have the other one," he said. "I'll hang it where the friend leaves her baby."

Maggie could not help herself; she was fascinated. She handed the yellow-dotted baby to Mitch, and he touched him to the crack. The infant's feet took a firm grip. Both batlets squeaked and walked around as if they knew something was wrong. Each was in a strange home. Hearing each other seemed to reassure them, however, and they finally settled down and went to sleep.

Maggie and Mitch sat down on the cot.

"I guess I've done enough for today," Mitch said after a while. "Let's go look for raven babies."

That evening Maggie, Mitch, and the Winters sat on the steps listening to the adult ravens quorking and yodeling in the valley. The birds kept up a patter of dongs and creaks that sounded like barn doors swinging in the wind.

"I wonder what they're saying," Grace said.

"Maybe they're sorry they sent their children away," suggested Maggie.

"I'll bet they're not," Andy said.

A fox crossed the meadow, three deer came out of the forest to browse in the tender grasses, and the robins sang the last carol of the day. But there were no sounds from the adolescent ravens.

Maggie went to her loft, changed the paper under the bats, and stretched out on her back to watch them. The wind blew leaves through the window. They scratched across the floor and then lay still. Grace poked her head above the loft floor.

"In bed?" she asked.

"Yes," Maggie said, staring at the baby bats. Both mothers were still gone. Both babies were still in the wrong places.

"Good," answered Grace. "Andy brought back sausages for breakfast."

"Yum," Maggie answered. Her eyes were still on the batlets. "Where's Mitch?"

"Andy's tucking him into bed out in the tent. Go to sleep. We'll be coming up soon." The Winters were using Evelyn and Fred's big double bed on the other side of the chimney.

Maggie set her alarm clock for an hour before sunrise and about the time the bats returned from hunting. Then she cuddled down under the comforter and went to sleep.

She awoke before the alarm went off and reached for her flashlight. The mother bats were home. Yellow dot was with yellow dot. White dot was with white dot. And the yellows were by the nail, the whites on the rafter.

"Of course your moms know you," she said smiling. "All moms know their babies."

She rolled onto her side so that she could see the adolescent fire bugs in the holding jars. They were quiet. The adults in the terrarium were also still. She thought how lucky she had been to have seen one metamorphose before they all turned into Peter Pans.

She sat bolt upright in bed.

"It's the holding jars," she said, and got to her feet. "Something's wrong with the holding jars. The one adolescent we left in the terrarium became an adult. The ones in the holding jars didn't."

She turned on her flashlight and stared at the three containers.

"What's different?" she asked herself. And then she knew. The paper! There was sand in the terrarium. The fire bugs had eaten the paper. They seemed very fond of it, as a matter of fact.

"The paper is the murderer," she said, taking out a piece riddled with bug holes. She looked at it through her magnifying glass.

"That's it. It's some chemical in the paper."

Maggie thought about waking Mitch and asking him to think of an experiment to prove that the paper had done it, but the night was cold, so she crawled back into bed.

We'll go to Rumford, she thought. Somebody at the Rumford Paper Mill will know what chemicals are used to make paper, and we can test each one. Mitch will have fun with that.

She could not sleep. Once more she got out of bed. This time she rummaged through her bureau drawer until she found a plastic box. She took one of the adolescents from the sandy-bottomed terrarium and put it in the plastic box, but with no paper.

"There," she said to herself. "I've got a control." Maggie had a terrarium with sand, and holding jars with paper. Now she had a clear plastic box with neither. If the little bug in the box became an adult like the one in the terrarium, she would know it was the paper.

The baby bats slept peacefully. They knew nothing about the experiment Mitch had devised to find out if their mothers recognized them.

Breathing deeply of the balsam-scented air, Maggie listened to the needles of the fir tree swish magically in the wind and remembered her promise to make Capek a pillow of balsam fir needles.

I'll have the mystery solved by the time he comes back, she thought. And thank goodness. What a terrible thing to do to a birthday present.

She slept well.

8

THE PAPER FACTOR

"It's the ozone hole," said Mitch, poking his head up over the floor of the loft long before the wood pewee sang.

Maggie lifted her head. Mitch's face, grinning just above the floor, made him look bodiless, like the Cheshire Cat. She blinked and put her head back on her pillow. Closing her eyes, she pretended she had not heard.

"I know it's the ozone hole." Mitch was now across from her, looking at the fire bugs. "The American Medical Association journal says 'Ultraviolet rays cause cataracts and cancer.'" Maggie did not open her eyes or move.

"The ozone layer protects us from ultraviolet rays. The holes don't. Hey, Maggie." He was standing above her. "The dictionary says cataracts obstruct passage of the waves of light. The bugs have gotten cataracts from ultraviolet radiation. Insect wings need light to develop—"

"Please, Mitch." Maggie threw off the quilt. "I'll get up. I'll get up."

"Or it could be the global warming from the greenhouse effect," he said. "Too hot—all their skins are coming off."

"Mitch," she said. "I know 'who done it.' I figured it out last night. Just take it easy."

A gust of cool air swirled through the window, and on it rode Myotis, home for the day. She flew to the nail on the rafter and took the baby under her wings.

"That's not her baby," said Mitch gleefully. "I've just proved bats raise any kid they come upon. First come first served."

"It is," said Maggie. "The mothers found their own babies early this morning."

"I switched them again about an hour ago while you were sleeping," said Mitch, quite pleased with himself.

Maggie scrambled up onto the stool; Myotis turned her head and looked down at her. The little brown bat opened her mouth but Maggie could not hear her sounds. She did see, however, that Myotis had a baby with a white dot. This time she had the wrong baby.

"When you have millions and millions of babies," said Maggie defensively, "and they're all hanging in a cave with millions and millions of mothers returning home all at once to take care of them, it just might be more sensible to fly as far as you can to the rear of the cave and take care of the first baby you find. Myotis has inherited this wisdom."

Maggie was not happy with this, but what else could she say? Myotis did have the wrong baby.

"That," said Mitch, "is what I've just proven." Sitting on the bed, with his cowlick sticking straight up in the cold air, he looked ridiculous, but very pleased with himself. Suddenly Myotis took off, carrying the wrong baby against her breast. Splinter took off with the other wrong baby. They met, fluttered, and when they came back to their home spots, each had her own baby.

"What I've just proven," said Mitch after watching this performance, "is that mother bats know their own babies."

"Whatever you say, Mitch," said Maggie, smiling.

"It's the ozone hole," he said.

"Whatever you say, except that." She shoved her

feet into her new boots and backed down the ladder. "Let's stoke the fire," she said. "Andy brought sausages for breakfast. I'll cook this morning."

"About the ozone hole," Mitch said, coming down behind her and dropping to the floor. "There's good ozone and bad ozone."

"Have you been at a computer already this morning?"

"Naturally," he said. "We've got to solve this thing before there are more murders. The computers will do it."

"Well, then," she said, "make them eat paper and tell us what's in it."

"As I was saying," he said, handing her a piece of kindling, "there is good ozone and bad ozone. They're both the same—a molecule made of three oxygen atoms. It's where they are that makes them good or bad." He sniffed the sausages Maggie was cooking and licked his lips.

"Last night," he went on, "I was wide awake so I got up and dialed into the university computer and got BIOLIN again." Mitch filled the water kettle and put it on the stove. "It said that this ozone is brewed in two places; down here on earth and up in the stratosphere. Down here ozone is made when sunlight cooks up an atmospheric stew of nitrogen oxides and hydrocarbons from automobiles and industry and other pollutants. It's bad only because it gives people and animals lung diseases and cancer."

"Well, that's pretty bad," said Maggie, getting down the hot chocolate mix.

Mitch ignored her.

"Ozone is good when it's up in the stratosphere." He looked at her to get her reaction to this wizardry. She turned the sausages without a comment.

"When it's up in the stratosphere," he repeated, "it protects us from ultraviolet rays that are deadly. Up there, the ozone is made by the sun's solar radiation and that ozone wraps itself around us like a shield—at least it did until we released chlorofluorocarbons that eat ozone. They went skyward and made huge holes in the ozone layer over Europe, the Antarctic, and now right over us."

"What's that got to do with my fire bugs dying before they grow up?"

"They will turn into adults if we stop using chlorine and bromine compounds in refrigerators, air conditioners, fire extinguishers"—he took a deep breath—"spray cans, and . . . other stuff on a long list I saw on BIOLIN." He rolled his eyes.

"Soon we'll all be Peter Pans like the fire bugs,"

he said. "They're a first warning to us like canaries in a mine that die and warn miners of dangerous gases in the air before they die."

"Nonsense," Maggie said. "Dad said we've already stopped making a lot of those chemicals that eat ozone." She opened the refrigerator and took out a carton of eggs.

"But the hole is still there," said Mitch, "and growing. It'll take a century for all the stuff we've already used to get up to the stratosphere—a century or more."

"I guess so," said Maggie cracking some eggs into a bowl.

"So I've got an idea," said Mitch. He heaped a tablespoon with hot chocolate mix and put it in a cup. "We can build big pipes from, say, Times Square in New York City to the stratosphere, and pipe the bad ozone up to make it good ozone."

"Well, for goodness' sakes!" exclaimed Andy as he came down the ladder. "Pipes to the stratosphere? I'm in the wrong world."

"No, you're not," Maggie said. "We are here on a mountain with a wood stove and a frying pan full of sausages."

"Aha," he said. "Now I understand what you're talking about." He chuckled. "Sausages—I am in the right world." He opened the folding table, set four places, and sat down.

"Andy," Mitch said enthusiastically, "do you want to see how we can pipe ozone from our cities up to the stratosphere and mend the holes up there?"

"I never thought I did until this moment," said Andy, scratching his chin, "but, yes, I guess I do." He smiled and stretched his arms and legs.

Mitch ran to the computer in the corner. "There's a modeler here," he called. "You can draw three-dimensional pictures on it—in color. Wait a second and I'll show you." Maggie asked Andy how he wanted his eggs and glanced at the computer screen. Colors came on the screen and took shape under Mitch's guidance.

Quork.

Maggie looked out the window. The raven was in the fir tree again. He seemed to have made it his own. She smiled. It was thrilling to have a raven so close, whether he was good or evil.

The door opened and Grace, who had gone home before the others were up, came in with a basket of blueberries.

"Good morning," she said. "It's nippy out." With her came a gust of fresh air laden with the piny scent of the balsam fir. Maggie breathed deeply and glanced at the tree. High in its branches the raven was now preening his feathers, lining them up for flight. The fir's lacy limbs moved gently, as if the tree were breathing. She had the eerie feeling, once again, that the fir was aware of her. She shook the thought from her head and told herself it was the raven that was making her feel that way. She knew trees weren't aware of anything.

When the four had finished eating, Andy pushed back his chair and wiped his mouth with a paper towel.

"Who wants to go to Rumford?" he asked. "I've got to deliver a load of wood there."

"I do," said Maggie, pleasantly surprised. "I was going to ask you when you'd be going there again. I really want to go."

"Fine," Andy said. "What about you, Mitch?" Maggie turned to look at him. Mitch was typing commands into the color computer.

"Can't get the pipes higher than a mile," he said, and got to his feet, leaving a gaudy three-dimensional drawing on the computer. "You going to Rumford, Maggie?"

"I want to go to the paper mill," she said.

"The paper mill—why the paper mill?"

"If you'd be quiet about the ozone hole for a moment, I'd tell you why."

"I'm quiet."

"It's perfectly obvious that some chemical in the paper is killing the fire bugs. The adolescents that eat paper become Peter Pans and die. Those that don't, become adults."

"That's too simple," he said, returning to the computer. "I prefer the ozone stuff." Maggie went up the ladder to get dressed in town clothes but stopped halfway.

"When you're finished with your ozone pipes, Mitch," she called from the ladder, "come up here, and I'll prove it."

"Those bugs," Grace said, as she cleared the table, "have certainly caused a commotion."

"You going, Grace?" Andy asked.

"No, I'll do the dishes and pick blueberries." She smiled at her husband. "You'll be glad I stayed home when Thanksgiving comes."

"What about you, Mitch?" Andy asked. The boy hesitated, then glanced at his diagram, richly colored in reds, blues, and greens.

"Oh, okay," he said. He didn't want to miss a ride to town. "I'll finish the pipes when I get back."

Quork!

The computer screen went blank. Mitch frowned and turned the machine off.

They had about an hour before Andy would be ready. Maggie went out to check her spider, and while she was gone Mitch climbed to the loft. He picked up first one holding jar, then the other. He studied the terrarium. He saw that the bugs that were eating the paper were all Peter Pans, but the bugs in the terrarium with no paper were all normal. He sat a long time looking at the fire bugs. Presently Maggie stuck her head above the loft floor.

"It's the paper," Mitch said. "But it's the chlorine in the paper. Paper is bleached with chlorine to make it white. I'll run a little test." He slipped past Maggie and went down to the lab, collected an eyedropper, a glass vial, and a bottle of bleach, and climbed back to the loft. With the eyedropper he obtained a small amount of chlorine bleach from the bottle and squeezed it into the vial.

"Mitch," Maggie said, "I checked Araneus. She's still holding on to the little piece of cork you gave her."

"That's kind of sad," he said.

"You were supposed to give her eggs back to her," she said crossly.

"Oh yeah, I was," he said. "Okay, I'll do it." He put a third-stage adolescent fire bug in the vial and held it up to the light.

"What are you doing?" Maggie cried.

"Testing the fire bugs for chlorine disease."

"Why, for heaven's sake?"

"You know why—to prove it's the chlorine in the paper that makes them Peter Pans." He looked at the vial. "See, the bug's dead."

"Mitch," she said in exasperation, "you just burned him to death with chlorine bleach. Please, don't do any more experiments until we talk to the people at the mill." She picked up her notebook and backed down the ladder.

"I would get an answer quicker if I stayed here," he said, following her. "I just got on-line access to the research files at the entomological station in Hamden, Connecticut."

"You did?" She turned around and stared at him. She did not remember her mother or dad telling her about that access. She put her hands on her hips. Things were not as they should be. The computers were baffling, Mitch was baffling, the raven was baffling, the fire bugs were baffling, even plain old paper was baffling—and yet, she thought, they are somehow all leading to the solution of the fire bug murders.

"Hear what I said?" asked Mitch. "I've gotten into the files at the entomological station at Hamden, Connecticut."

"I heard you," Maggie answered. "Look at them when you get back. I need your help. I don't understand chemicals."

"Oh, all right," he said, as pleased as a bat in a caddis fly hatch. He ran to his tent to change into clean trousers and a shirt.

Andy was in his wood truck waiting for them when they reached the road. The day was bright and clear, the air sweet with wilderness scents of loam, pines, and moist fungi. Maggie was thoughtful as the truck rolled down the mountain. She would soon find the villain who killed the fire bugs before they could grow up.

As they cut through Blueberry Mountain Pass, Andy slowed down the truck and came to a stop. He pointed to a clearing in the forest. Twenty or thirty ravens were yelling and jumping up and down.

"Wow," said Maggie. "Look at all the ravens. What are they doing?"

The birds leaped onto their wings, turned loops, and yelled. With each raucous cry, more ravens came out of the forest and joined the mob. Andy lifted his binoculars to his eyes.

"They've got a big moose carcass," he said, passing the binoculars to Maggie, who was seated in the middle. "Sometimes when ravens find a carcass, they call in all their friends to dine. Sometimes they don't."

"You mean," Mitch said, "ravens share? I thought only people did that."

"It's sharing, but for a selfish reason," said Andy. He paused to think. "Which is also why people share, I guess. We hope to get like treatment or to make ourselves feel good, which is sort of selfish. But the ravens? Why do they share?"

"For the same reasons?" asked Mitch.

"Almost," said Andy. "A man named Bernd Heinrich, down near Dixfield, has been studying ravens for years. He's a professor from Vermont. He told me a lot about ravens." He turned to Maggie. "You saw the raven parents of the creek canyon chase their kids away, didn't you?"

"Yes," she answered. "It was cruel. They were hungry."

"Well, Bernd Heinrich says the young can get in on a big food source like a moose or deer, if they call in their young friends who have no homes or territories, like that young raven who dives at you, Maggie. They overwhelm the pair who own the territory the carcass is on and force them to share."

"Well, that's smart," said Mitch. "I'll remember that."

"The parents aren't sharing," said Maggie. "It's the young. They're calling in their friends and making the adults share."

"Same result," said Andy. "Everybody eats."

"I wonder if our young ravens are here?" Maggie suddenly asked, craning her neck to see.

"I wouldn't be surprised." Andy said.

"We should have put poster paint on them," said Mitch. "Then we'd know."

Quork.

Mitch leaned out the window. A large raven sat in a tree, a few feet from his head.

"Another fire bug bit the dust," he said. He grinned and poked Maggie.

"I guess we know better than that," she said as she watched the gang of young ravens dancing and jumping and yodeling. "But ravens still mean death. A moose has fallen."

"They didn't kill it," said Mitch.

"But they told Andy a moose was dead," Maggie said, thinking of what her grandmother had said.

"What they really told me," said Andy, "was where I could find food. If I had been starving,

Raven would have meant life."

Maggie liked that idea. "The Native Americans are right," she said. "Raven is life. Grandmother never had to survive in the forest."

"They're also rascals," said Mitch.

"Why do you say that?" Maggie asked.

"That one at the lab," Mitch answered. "I was quietly watching the fire bugs this morning," he said, "and Raven came in the window and took your comb off the shelf. He stole it."

"Mitch, you're making that up," said Maggie. "He would never come in the window, even if you were under a blanket."

"I was—at least I was wrapped in one. It was cold." He looked worriedly out the window. "And, another thing about that rascal: When Raven's on the roof or in the fir tree, I get BIOLIN strong and clear. When he's not, it does funny things and it crashes."

"Raven is powerful," said Andy. Maggie glanced from one to the other and said no more.

Just outside Rumford the road ran along the Androscoggin River. Maggie watched it closely, looking for signs of pollution as they neared the paper mill. Paper mills, she knew, were one of the most deadly of the big industries. They spewed cancer-causing chloroform, a by-product of papermaking, into the atmosphere, and chlorine into the rivers. She was surprised to see that the Androscoggin looked clear. Then she remembered her father saying the mill was making a great effort to clean up the river. Cleaning the air was more difficult; the sky became gray-brown and smelly as they drove into Rumford and stopped at a traffic light.

"If you'll help me unload this wood," Andy said, "I'll go with you to the paper mill." He shifted into first gear. "I'd like to see that operation."

"And, I'd like to see what chemicals are murdering my fire bugs in the cruelest of all possible ways," said Maggie.

"We don't need to go any farther," said Mitch. He sniffed and then held his nose. "I know what's murdering them—chloroform—smell it? I'm dying! The villain is here."

Maggie rolled her eyes and said, "Oh, Mitch, we all know there's no chloroform in paper. You're just being dramatic."

9
THE PULP

The Rumford Paper Mill was an enormous complex of buildings, smokestacks, towers, and rails taking up almost half a mile of land on the river's edge. The town rose around it on both sides of a steep valley. On the hilltop, splendid houses faced away from the mill to the White Mountains of New Hampshire and the grizzled foothills of Maine. Below them the workers' narrow homes were hunched in the perpetual gloom of the mill smog. Andy drove slowly into town.

"Paper's gotta be mighty important to this country," he said, looking at the massive mill on the other side of the river. "I guess the amount we use in one day would wrap up the Earth for Christmas."

Trucks stacked with logs snaked down the mountain roads heading for the mill. Along the river, log-laden railroad cars inched toward the hungry tree eater.

"Lots of trees," said Mitch, after counting trucks and flatcars.

"Lots and lots," said Andy.

"Do they all come from Maine?"

"Once they all came from Maine, but now the mill has to go to Canada for trees."

"I hope they replant," Mitch said.

"Most companies do," said Andy. "Trees are a crop like corn. Paper companies eat them, so paper companies grow them."

"My dad," said Mitch, looking out at the scraggly trees on the surrounding mountains, "told me you have to plant right away or the soil will erode and the next generation of trees will be stunted."

"Some companies plant right away," said Andy.

"Does that mean that a lot don't?" asked Maggie.

"When I go out to collect wood for my firewood business," Andy answered, "I see miles of eroded mountains. Miles."

As they joined the slow march of trucks at the bottom of a hill, Andy reached into the glove compartment for a map. He handed it to Maggie.

"I'm looking for twenty-seven Beaver Street," he said. She bent over the map. Mitch leaned out the window as they came to a stop behind a truckload of limbless tree trunks.

"What kind of trees are those?" he asked.

"Balsam fir," Andy replied. "Most all the paper we use is made from balsam fir—newsprint, slick magazine paper—you name it, it's balsam fir pulp."

Maggie looked up.

"Balsam fir?" She thought of the tall slender tree by the cabin that treated her with bursts of scent when the wind blew. She was glad it was safe from the woodchoppers.

"Turn right at the next traffic light," she said. "Beaver Street is two blocks up."

The houses on Beaver Street were small and plain, and many needed repairs and paint.

"It gets mighty smoky in this section of town in the winter," Andy said as he turned into the yard of 27 Beaver Street. "All these people have wood furnaces." He backed up beside the house and stopped. Maggie and Mitch watched him throw a lever on his truck. The dumper began to rise, and the wood clattered and rumbled as it slid to the ground.

"Now we stack," Andy said, getting down from the cab.

The back door of the house opened, and an elderly man hobbled out.

"Good morning," Andy called. "You must be Chet, the one I talked to on the telephone?"

"No, that was my son. I'm Clive. He told me to pay you." Clive handed him a roll of bills, which Andy counted.

"All here," Andy said, then added, "I'm taking my young friends here to the mill after we stack. Know anyone there who might show us around?"

"I worked at the mill for forty years," Clive said, ignoring the question. "Ran the hydraulic barker that stripped the logs naked. Used to get the bark for my furnace. No more. The company uses the bark for its power plant."

"Know what chemicals they put in the paper?" Andy asked. "These kids want to know."

"Didn't use any chemicals where I worked. The logs were cut into three-foot lengths, and I put them on a conveyor belt that took them to the chipper."

Maggie carried a log to the woodpile, then eagerly joined Andy to listen to Clive.

"In eleven seconds that chipper disintegrated those logs into little one-inch chips. Eleven seconds. Think of that. A big log to dust in eleven seconds. That chipper blade spun so fast, you'd couldn't see it. You'd just see the log vanish."

"Did they put the chips in a chemical?" Maggie asked.

"No," Clive answered. "We put the chips on a conveyor belt that took them to the digester. It's like a huge pressure cooker three stories high. The heat and pressure is tremendous in that cooker. Seven hours later my son, Chet—he works on the digester—opens the door, and mush falls out."

"Mush?" said Mitch. "Do they put chemicals in the mush?"

"Well," Clive said, "the mush goes to big tanks where huge paddle wheels break up the fiber. Next it goes on another conveyor belt to the bleaching plant, where the gray-brown color is taken out of it. Here's where a chemical comes in."

"What is it?" Maggie asked eagerly.

"Chlorine."

"Oh," said Mitch, glancing at Maggie. "But the chlorine must evaporate. There's none left in the paper or you'd smell it."

"Yup, that's right," said Clive. "Most of it anyway."

"Is that all they add?" asked Maggie.

"That's all. Then it goes in a big ten-inch pipe to the paper foundry—which is as big as a football field. A giant machine rolls it and takes out the water. Then it's a hundred percent air-dried."

"Nothing else is used to dry it, like a chemical?" Maggie persisted.

"Nope. When the big sheets are dry, they're pure white pulp from the tree—cardboard. They're cut into huge sheets, bound into bales, five hundred pounds a piece, and loaded on a flatcar for the paper mill. Sixty tons of cardboard goes out on each flatcar, day after day after day."

"That's a lot of trees," said Andy.

"A mountainside a day," Clive said raising his eyebrows.

Maggie was not giving up. "What chemicals do they use to make the paper?"

"They add clay—real clay from Virginia—to make that slick magazine paper. Rag is added to make real good paper like the paper for paper money."

"Is the clay harmful?" Maggie asked.

"Nah," Clive answered. "My kids used to play with it."

Maggie put a last log on the woodpile and got in the cab. Mitch climbed in beside her.

"That clue is blasted," Maggie said to him. "The chemicals they use in paper couldn't make Peter Pans. What am I going to tell Capek when he sees what's happening to his present?"

The old man walked with Andy to the truck.

"Go to the main office," he said. "Ask for Harry. He gives tours of the plant. Tell him I sent you.

He's a nice man. He'll help the kids."

"Thank you," said Andy. "We just might do that. But first we're going to eat. Know any good places for kids?"

"Paul Bunyan's on Maine Street serves a good burger," he said. "And it's cheap."

Andy nodded his thanks and drove off.

"Chlorine, and clay," Maggie said slowly, "and tree pulp equals paper."

"You still think it's the paper?" asked Mitch.

"Don't you?"

"Yes," he said. "Those fire bugs that ate paper are Peter Pans. Those that didn't are adults. But what else can it be if it's not chemicals?"

"I don't know." Maggie thought a moment, then swung around and faced Mitch.

"The pulp," she said. "That's all that's left."

Mitch thought a moment, then frowned. "You mean the tree?" he asked incredulously.

"I mean the tree."

"The tree did it?"

"Yes." She brushed a strand of pale blond hair from her cheek. "The tree did it."

"The tree is a murderer?"

"Yes."

"Aw, come on, Maggie," Mitch said. "Murder is killing on purpose."

"Well?"

"You mean the tree wanted to kill the fire bugs before they had young? Come on. Trees can't plot a murder."

"Well, you think about it," she said.

He slumped back in the seat and stared at the trees on the mountainside.

"Yeah," he said slowly. "Bugs kill trees. So trees kill bugs; and they don't just kill them, they kill them before they can lay eggs. Wow. Wait till Capek hears this."

"He'll love it," Maggie said. "But we're not done."

Mitch thought a moment. "Back to BIOLIN?"

"I think so," she said. "There must be some entomologists who know what makes insects grow up or stop growing up."

"And the tree knows it too?"

"The tree knows it too."

"This is spookier than ravens," said Mitch. He leaned back in his seat and slumped down again, thinking.

"Wow," he murmured. "The tree did it." He looked at Maggie. She looked back at him.

"Makes sense to me," said Andy. "Trees are very ancient. They've had a lot of time to figure things out."

He looked at the two children, who were staring at him with large thoughtful eyes.

"I'm starved," he said. "Let's eat." He turned the truck onto Maine Street. "After we eat, I want to see that chipper—eleven seconds and a tree is chips." He pulled into the Paul Bunyan parking lot.

"Eleven seconds," he repeated. "That's unbelievable."

"Not as unbelievable as a tree that can plot and carry out a diabolical murder," Maggie said.

"You're right," said Andy as he helped her down from the cab. "That's out of our world altogether."

10
THE MURDER WEAPON

Maggie mused as she climbed the hill to the laboratory. The trip through the factory had been unforgettable. Whole trees had vanished, pulp had boiled, paper had formed before her eyes—and she had found the villain.

The balsam fir came into view, perfect, slender, and now more mysterious than ever. It knew how to keep fire bugs from growing up and multiplying—but how?

The tree had always been a presence to her, nodding to her on her birthday, sheltering ravens, and wafting its scent into her room. Today it was more than that. The movement of its branches and its odor were, she thought, the brain waves of a great thinker. Some intelligence was inside that fir, locked into the bark and cambium, into the cellulose and resin, into the needles. It was an otherworldly intelligence that no human being would ever fathom. Somehow that tall, slender tree had figured out how to prevent little fire bug adolescents from ever growing up. They would die before they had young.

"That's horrible," she said to the balsam fir.

Quork, quark. The raven sailed out of the forest and alighted on the fir. He began pecking the branch, and the noise rat-a-tatted through the mountains.

"No, raven, no!" she shouted. "I didn't mean it. It's a wonderful tree." The raven pecked on, his beak flipping bits of bark to the ground. Mitch, who was close behind Maggie, stopped and stared at the bird.

"What's wrong with him?" he asked.

"I just said that the tree was horrible, and he flew in and started beating it up."

"Wow," said Mitch. "I'm getting out of here. First you tell me a tree can commit murder, then you tell me a raven can seek revenge. Weeeird." He flung open the lab door and headed for the computers.

Maggie knew better than to think the raven understood what she had said, so she slowly turned in a circle to see what effect the drumming was having on the forest wildlife. Obviously this noisy rat-a-tat was a message to someone.

Far down the valley five ravens were flying off into the distance, beating their wings and then gliding.

She wondered who they were. Too many to be the creek canyon youngsters. Perhaps they were the young of some other pair that had been driven from home and were out scouting for food. They had trespassed, and the raven on the fir was warning them to move on. And they were going—swiftly, silently.

Maggie watched the strangers until they had disappeared.

Suddenly the raven in the fir let out a scream, sounding like a dog whose tail had been stepped on. Still screaming, he flew out of the tree and began climbing above the cabin. High, high in the marine-blue sky of late summer, he rolled onto his back and flew upside down. His flight feathers pressed against a spiraling wind, and he was shot upward and out of sight. He called, then reappeared upside down, spiraled, flew right side up, twisted, and sailed down. He was more wonderful to watch than a stunt plane. He landed on the roof.

"Got it!" shouted Mitch from inside the lab.

"Got BIOLIN again. Is Raven back?"

Maggie stared at the raven. "Don't say that, Mitch," she whispered. "Computers are spooky enough without having a raven turn them on and off." The bird cocked an eye at her, lifted his crest, and flew off into the forest.

She ran inside. "Do you still have BIOLIN?" she called as she crossed the lab to the computers.

"No," he said, spinning around in his chair. "I just turned it off."

"You did?"

"Yeah, I want to work on the ozone pipes."

Maggie breathed a sigh of relief and started the fire in the stove for dinner, then climbed the ladder to the loft. She wanted to think all by herself.

She picked up the holding jars, held one in each hand, and sat down on her cot. Every red-and-black larva was fat. They were fifth-stage larvae and still not adults. She looked closely. One was a giant sixth-stage larva. All their wings were nubbins, and their steps were sluggish. They were approaching death with no offspring to carry on when they were gone. Maggie wished that removing the paper would help the little flame bugs recover and mature. But it was too late. The balsam fir had worked its crime.

She looked out at the tree and remembered she had promised Capek a pillow of needles to take back to the Czech and Slovak Federal Republic. She would spread a bed sheet in the sun and pile balsam fir branches on it. In a few days, when the needles dried and fell off, she would gather them and stuff a pillow.

She heard a squeak. Maggie looked up. Myotis was hanging far away from her yellow-dotted baby. Maggie had never seen her do this before. She was always with him. Was the little bat sick? Was Myotis sick? She looked at white-dotted Splinter, then back to Myotis. Her friend still had her mark, but Myotis did not have hers.

She looked again. Then she realized that the bat hanging alone was not Myotis at all, but a stranger. She tilted her head and smiled. Here was more evidence to show why biologists must mark the birds and animals they were studying. If Mitch hadn't painted dots on them, she would have made a note saying Myotis was no longer caring for her baby.

"Now I know what's happening," she said to the bats. "Autumn is coming. You little brown bats gather together to hibernate for the winter. Soon there will be lots of you in my loft."

She got up and replaced the holding jars.

She glanced up at the bats. She would not need a calendar or a clock if she knew enough about nature. The bats told her that this day was almost the end of August, and the wood pewee told her when the sun would rise.

Feeling pleased with this knowledge, she went to the window to see if she could add one more thing to her calendar—the smell of autumn. It should be sweet and dry like hay. She sniffed. The raven alighted on the roof. He cocked his head and came toward her.

"Maggie!" Mitch's voice was urgent. She zipped down the ladder.

"BIOLIN again. I got the biological data files," he said. "Listen to this article in *Scientific American*. It's on pesticides; July nineteen sixty-seven. Volume two seventeen, number three: 'The prime candidate for developing new pesticides is the juvenile hormone that all insects secrete at certain stages in their lives. It is one of the three internal secretions used by insects to regulate growth and metamorphosis from larva to pupa to adult. In the living insect a juvenile hormone is synthesized by two tiny glands in the head.'"

"So?" Maggie said.

"Well, wait a second," Mitch said. "'At certain stages the hormone must be secreted; at certain stages it must be absent or the insect will develop abnormally.'"

"Go on," Maggie said stepping closer.

"'In order for a larva to metamorphose into a sexually mature adult, the flow of the hormone must stop. Still later, after the adult is formed, juvenile hormone must again be secreted.'"

"Let me see that," Maggie said. She leaned over the computer and read aloud: "'In order for a larva to metamorphose into a sexually mature adult, the flow of the hormone must stop.'"

"It didn't stop, did it?" asked Mitch.

"I guess not." She looked out the window. "Somehow that tree manufactures a hormone, and the fire bugs keep getting it when they eat paper—or the tree."

"That makes sense," said Mitch. Maggie sat down beside him. He pressed a key, and the beginning of the article reappeared. They carefully reread the first paragraph.

Suddenly there was only half a page on the screen.

"Nuts," Mitch said, clicking keys and trying commands. Then the computer crashed. The screen went blank. He snapped his fingers and ran to the window.

"What's wrong?" Maggie called.

"The raven," he said. "The raven's gone."

"Oh, Mitch," she said. "It's just a coincidence. That's just too weird. A raven can't make a computer go on and off."

"Yeah?" Mitch replied. "If a tree can make a hormone, a raven can crash a computer. He's a rascal. Remember?" He sat down at another of the three computers.

"This one works," he said. "I'll try to get the computer at the U.S. Department of Insect Investigations at Hamden again." He watched the screen intently.

"Ask it what else a tree knows," Maggie said. The computer whirred softly.

"I'm asking it for everything it has on insect juvenile hormones."

Nothing came up, so Mitch darkened the screen, but left it on. He moved to the color computer and opened up the file where he had stored his ozone pipe drawing. He waited.

"I wonder if there are any balsam firs where the fire bugs came from," he said to Maggie.

"No," she answered. "Capek said there weren't. And we've answered his question about why fire bugs can't live in New England."

"The balsam firs murder them all," said Mitch.

"Exactly," said Maggie.

"I wish my father would get here," Mitch said. "This is important. He might know how the tree does it."

Maggie put a pot of beans on the stove to heat up for supper, then walked outside and sat down on the step. Mitch joined her. The crickets were stridulating, and a monarch butterfly was sipping nectar from a goldenrod before migrating to Mexico. The two were quiet for a long time. Finally Maggie stood up.

"Help me cut some balsam fir limbs, will you, Mitch?" she asked. "Capek wants a pillow."

"Me, too," he said picking a twig from the raven's fir tree as they passed by it. He stuck it in his mouth.

"Better be careful," Maggie chided. "You'll stop growing and pop."

He laughed. "You're as crazy as a fire bug!" But he spit out the twig.

For two days Maggie and Mitch kept watch on the fire bugs in the paperless terrarium, and were pleased with their detective work. The last two larvae metamorphosed and, in flaming red colors, became adults. Maggie and Mitch had solved the mystery, and the birthday gift would survive.

Several evenings before Expedition North Woods returned, three more bats joined Myotis and her friend. The following day the wasp crept into the grasses and died. Her work was done. Her eggs were in her nest deep in the ground, carefully embedded in the crickets and grasshoppers they would dine upon when they hatched. Next spring her progeny would grow up, develop wings, and fly out into the sunshine.

Araneus, the spider, was forgotten for several days. Andy took Maggie and Mitch fishing by day, and in the evening Mitch taught Maggie how to use the computer while Andy marveled. When Maggie was on her own with the word processor program, Mitch played a computer game with Grace, who caught on very quickly. He had made and programmed it himself, so he was a bit embarrassed when Grace beat him at his own game.

One afternoon Grace asked Maggie to play Mitch's game with her while Mitch climbed the ladder to check on the fire bugs. Beautiful adults flew, mated, and laid eggs. There would be more fire bugs.

Before returning to the lab, Mitch stood at the window to look at the mysterious balsam fir. The raven was back. He was on the roof walking slowly downward, his head bobbing. Mitch fairly jumped down the ladder and turned on the computer to the university. BIOLIN came on the screen.

"Now what are you doing?" Maggie asked.

"Go outside and see if that raven is twisting a phone wire or something," Mitch said. "This computer really does seem to work when the raven's here and not work when he's gone."

"Oh, Mitch," she said in exasperation, but she went outside and looked up.

"He's not here," she called. "If that helps."

"It does," he shouted back. "It just crashed."

"Really?" Maggie came inside and stood close to Andy. "Mitch is getting cabin fever," she said. "He thinks Raven runs the computers."

"Wonderful bird," Andy said. "Raven probably created computers. After all, he created the Earth and the sun and the moon."

"And the bats and bugs," added Mitch.

"And the trees," said Andy.

Maggie put her hands to her head to close out these thoughts, then took them down. She looked at Mitch.

"I know one thing for sure about Raven," she said.

"What?" asked Mitch.

"He's a rascal. You are right about that."

"Now what?" asked Mitch.

"I found my comb."

"Where was it?"

"In the watering can." She looked at him.

"I didn't do it!" he exclaimed. "I didn't do it!"

"I know it," said Maggie smiling puckishly. "I know very well you didn't do it. All the ski pins from your jacket were in the watering can too."

"No!" cried Mitch running out the back door. "My pins—they'll rust. That's a dirty trick!"

"You should know," called Maggie, and chuckled as she went back to her game with Grace.

"No wonder the balsam fir is smart," she said to the Winters. "Raven created it." Andy nodded.

"Now you're catching on," he said, warming his hands at the stove. "Now, you're catching on."

11

THE FIRE BUG CONNECTION

When the North Woods Expedition returned to Bug Camp, they greeted Maggie and Mitch warmly and thanked Grace and Andy for their help. For several hours they recounted the tale of the black bear that had come into camp and licked sleeping Capek's bare foot, startling both him and the bear. Fred told about the terrible fish soup Jim Waterford had made and the skunk that adopted them and came every night for a handout. "We didn't refuse him," said Evelyn.

It was not until everyone was seated around the table for dinner that Capek asked Maggie if the fire bugs were all right.

"All but a few in the terrarium have died," she answered.

"Really?" he said. "Why? Do you know?"

"It was murder," she answered. "Premeditated murder."

Capek laughed jovially, and Jim shifted his feet to express amusement.

"It was," said Mitch, coming to Maggie's defense.

"Well, well," said Jim, patting his son condescendingly on the head as if to say he was a good boy but very young and full of nonsense.

"I guess," said Maggie's dad, "I must be the one to ask 'who done it?'"

"The tree," said Mitch.

"The balsam fir," said Maggie.

"I wish the trees could get rid of the acid rain that easily," Evelyn said, and chuckled.

"Let's go over the evidence," said Fred, glad to get his mind off the strenuous trip that was now behind him. A fire bug murder was just the diversion he needed.

"Can you tell me what happened?" he asked Maggie.

"It's fairly simple," she said. "The fire bugs that ate the paper in the holding jars didn't grow up. The ones that didn't eat paper became adults. We decided it was a chemical in the paper, and Andy took us to the paper mill to find out what chemicals are used to make paper."

"What are they?" asked Capek.

"None, except chlorine, and that evaporates when the paper is made. So there was only one thing left."

"What?" said Fred. "I'm holding my breath."

"Pulp," said Maggie.

"Or, in other words, the tree," said Mitch.

Maggie looked from one I-don't-believe-it face to the other, then hurried to the loft ladder.

"I'll bring the fire bugs down and show you," she said, and climbed out of sight. Mitch, seeing the raven fly to the roof, slipped out from under his father's hand and turned on a computer and punched a few keys. BIOLIN came on.

"I'm right," he said. "Raven's spooked the computers." Then he looked at the screen. He was getting an answer to his insect hormone query.

Maggie returned with the terrarium and went back for the two holding jars. She put the plastic box in her pocket.

"Now don't say anything," she said, looking from one amused face to the other, "until you've looked at all three containers. I'm sorry to say most of the Peter Pans in the holding jars are dead."

"Murdered by a tree?" said Capek, still thinking his little hostess was playing an entomological game that he was going to enjoy immensely. "Okay," he said. "I'll study them very carefully."

Capek laughed pleasantly, but not very long. He looked from the holding jars to the terrarium then quickly pulled up a chair, took out his magnifying glass, and studied the chewed paper and the sixth-stage larvae. He looked back at the terrarium. Evelyn leaned over his shoulder. Fred got to his feet, and Jim put down his fork. They joined Capek and Evelyn at the exhibits.

"I think the children are right," said Capek. "It does seem that something in the paper is arresting the development of the fire bugs and killing them. Interesting."

Jim Waterford was no longer being condescending. He was thoughtfully studying the evidence from all angles, bending lower and lower as he beheld a murder of the most sophisticated sort.

"But," he said, straightening to his full height, "there is no control here—just bugs on paper and bugs on sand. There are none in a sterile environment."

"That's true," said Fred. "Is it too late to put an adolescent from the terrarium in a paperless and sandless environment?"

"I'm afraid," said Capek, scrutinizing the terrarium carefully, "that it's too late. There are no more adolescent larvae here."

"Too bad," said Evelyn. "This is thrilling if it is true." She picked up the holding jar and studied it carefully.

"It is true," said Maggie, "and I can prove it." She reached into her pocket and took out the plastic box.

"Here's the control," she said. "I put this little bug in this box with no paper, no sand, and not even blueberries that might be tainted. I gave her bananas. And look, she turned into a perfect adult."

A murmur went around the room as the North Woods Expedition passed the box from one to the other, speculating and discussing. They finally all agreed it was so. Fred slipped his arm around his daughter and squeezed her. "Nice going," he said.

"What are the chemicals in paper?" asked Jim.

"Really none," said Maggie. "Clay—but that's harmless."

"It can't be clay," said Capek, "that turns them into—"

"—Peter Pans," said Maggie.

Evelyn walked to the window and looked at the tree. She blew it a kiss. "It hardly looks like a murderer," she said, "but if so, it is a beautiful one." Fred and Jim looked up balsam firs in their reference books to see if there was any mention of a tree killing insects. They found none.

"We've got the victim and the murderer," Evelyn said, coming back to the terrarium. "But we don't have the murder weapon."

Quark, quark. The raven had returned.

"We do!" shouted Mitch from the computer. "We do. Here's BIOLIN again." Maggie's spine tingled. Raven was back. Could Mitch be right about his computer powers?

"Read this article from *Scientific American,*" Mitch said excitedly.

"Read fast," he said. "BIOLIN isn't very stable. Keeps coming and going; but if someone would throw that raven a chunk of meat, you might have time to read this."

"What's the raven got to do with it?" Fred asked.

"It seems to me," said Mitch, "that it comes on when he's here, and goes off when he's gone."

"Oh, Mitch," Evelyn said. "It's not the raven. That computer has a virus. I didn't think to tell you because you were using the other one."

"Oho," said Mitch. He grinned. "So that's it—a virus—I'm very glad to know that. I feel a whole lot better."

"I wrote for a disinfectant to get rid of it," Evelyn

said. "But it hasn't come yet."

Maggie gasped. "A disinfectant?"

"A software disk that corrects the glitch, or as computer experts say, the 'virus.'" She laughed. "Does sound like computers are people; but that's the terminology."

Mitch waited patiently for the images to return, and presently BIOLIN reappeared.

"Listen to this," he called. "Scientists at the University of Wisconsin isolated and identified the murder weapon—that juvenile hormone. And its empirical formula is $C_{18}H_{36}O_2$, corresponding to a molecular weight of two eighty-four, whatever that means."

"A great deal," said Capek, rushing to Mitch's side. "This murder weapon—as you call it—is very significant. Very significant." He turned to Jim and Fred. "The children may have found the perfect way to control insects. Reproduce the juvenile hormone of each pest—they are all different—and spray it on their food. What is important about such a pesticide is that it won't kill anything else, only the insect it's designed for."

"It's quite a breakthrough," said Fred.

Capek began reading the *Scientific American* article from the beginning, and Mitch got up to let him sit down. He picked up a software disk and went to the third computer.

"This opens a new career for me," said Capek, staring at the screen. "Juvenile hormones as pesticides." He read the article once more.

"And here's what it looks like," called Mitch, pointing to a three-dimensional drawing of $C_{18}H_{36}O_2$. "It also kills with a pop," he added jubilantly. He got to his feet and stuck his hands in his pockets.

Suddenly he screamed. "Yikes! Yikes!"

"What's wrong?" Maggie asked, as he whirled around the room batting one hand with the other.

"I don't know!" he cried. "I'm creeping with things. I'm alive with wiggles."

Maggie grabbed his hands and looked at them.

"Mitch!" she exclaimed. "You never returned Araneus's eggs. You said you would. But you didn't. You put them in your pocket."

"I lost them," Mitch said. "Honest. I couldn't remember what I did with them."

"Well, *they* did," Maggie said, looking at hundreds of little spiders climbing and spinning on Mitch's arms and trousers. "And they hatched in your nice warm pocket." She began to laugh.

Mitch looked down at the spiderlings and laughed, too.

"Now what do I do?" he said, running out the door.

"Return them," Maggie said, following him.

"And don't return them just anywhere," she yelled as he headed for the woods. "Come back! They live in meadows and gardens." Mitch turned around.

"And you can't release them close together. They'll eat each other. They're predators, you know," Maggie said. Mitch brushed a few off his pants.

"Now, move over here," she said, and led him away from the others. When she was certain Mitch had released the last tiny daughter and son of Araneus, Maggie sat down under the balsam fir.

Mitch slumped beside her. "I always seem to learn about nature the hard way," he said.

"What do you mean?" she asked. "What else has happened?"

"The wasp," he said.

"What did you do?"

"She went off into the grass to die."

"They do that when they've laid all their eggs."

"I thought you said they didn't sting."

"Well, if you pick them up or something," she said, "I guess they might."

"They do," said Mitch, and showed her a large

red spot on his thumb.

"Good experiment, Mitch," she said. "I'll put that in my notes. Did she bite you or stick you with the stinger on her tail?"

He cast her a scornful glance and arose. "I'm going to try to cure the virus in the computer without the disinfectant. I know a few tricks." He went into the lab.

Maggie stretched out under the tree. Its branches moved gently in the cool air.

"Hello," she said. "I was right all the time. I knew you were more than a dumb tree." The limbs dipped and rose.

"Can you mix something to purify the acid rain, restore the ozone hole, and eat the carbon dioxide and methane that hold the heat from the sun against the earth and warm the atmosphere?"

Over her thoughts she heard Capek's voice through the open window.

"The juvenile hormone in the balsam fir," he said, "opens up a whole new source of insecticides."

"The trees?" Fred asked him.

"The trees," said Capek.

"I would suggest," said Jim, "that we look primarily at the evergreens. They are very ancient. They were here on earth before the insects. They are pollinated by the winds and, unlike other plants, do not depend on insects for anything. They can afford to kill them.

"There are thousands of other terpenoid materials," he went on, "that evergreen trees manufacture—for no apparent reason, we thought—until now. Perhaps this discovery of the fire bug connection will provoke us to find out what else these materials do."

"Yes," said Capek. "There is so much we do not know."

The scientists moved away from the window, and Maggie could not hear any more. She was glad. She was alone in the spell of the scented tree and its miraculous intelligence. She wanted to think about it by herself.

Quork, quark. The raven was jumping downward from limb to limb. He stopped not far above her. Out of the corner of her eye she could see the light from the computer reflected in the window glass. The BIOLIN program was on.

"Despite what Mom says about the virus," she said to the bird, "you seem to be connected to wonders. You are here when the program is on."

She sat up. There was one other thing she must test. Capek had said her pale-blond hair attracted the bird. She took out her Swiss army knife and cut off a lock. Holding it high, she dangled it before the raven. He sidled along a branch and jumped to a limb near her hand. He yodeled his note of pleasure. Cautiously he leaned down, then quickly took the lock from her fingers. He flew over the lab and out of sight.

Maggie jumped to her feet and ran pell-mell down the hill to find Andy. He was weeding his garden. She ran right up to him.

"Raven did want my hair," she said. "I cut some off to see if what Capek had said was true. He came right to my hand and took it." She smiled, very pleased that a raven had wanted her hair. "What will he do with it?" she asked.

Andy straightened up and leaned on his hoe. "Throw it into the sky to make a comet," he said, squinting at the heavens.

"I like that," she said. "I think that's beautiful."

A sudden wind came up, and Maggie was almost overwhelmed by the strong scent of the balsam fir.

"That smell reminds me," she said. "I haven't finished Capek's pillow. He'll truly want it now."

She ran up through the meadow and around the lab, her hair blending with the thistledown blowing on the autumn wind.

Maggie dropped to her knees on a sheet and began to shake dry needles from the fir limbs she and Mitch had collected. Tentatively she looked back at the lab. The computer screen was still lit. She smiled.

From far down the valley a raven called. She stood up and looked for him in the blue mountains and red clouds. He was not to be seen.

"Raven," she called into the emptiness. "You are very powerful. Andy is right. New discoveries were unfolded while you were with us—that the balsam fir can protect itself, that bats love their babies, that wasps can memorize, and a spider can't darn."

"*And*," shouted Mitch, jumping out of the tall grass and crooking his fingers above his head like a demon, "that computer viruses can be cured without a disinfectant." He smirked. "I did it."

"Mitch!" Maggie gasped. "You scared me." He laughed. Maggie leaned toward the valley.

"And one more thing, Raven," she called, cupping her hand around her mouth. "You and Mitch Waterford are rascals."

"Bah," he said, holding up his purple vest. "You can darn a web. Can you darn cloth?" he asked.

Maggie saw the holes where Raven had pulled the ski pins from the vest. "What an honor,

Mitch," she said, taking the vest and holding it up. "You must be the only person in the world who has a vest torn by a raven."

Mitch cocked his head, stepped back, and looked at it. "Yeah," he said. "Wow, you're right. It is pretty neat—raven holes." He slipped on his vest and strutted a bit, then stopped.

"Raven!" he called. "I left a Saint Moritz pin on the roof for you. Have a nice winter."

Laughing, Maggie and Mitch dropped to their knees to stuff the balsam needles into two small pillowcases.

Raven called from far away.

Summer was over.